CRUISING IN LOVE

A SWEET FEEL-GOOD ROMANCE

S J CRABB

Copyright © S J Crabb 2021

S J Crabb has asserted her rights under the Copyright, Designs and Patents Act 1988 to be identified as the Author of this work.

This book is a work of fiction and except in the case of historical fact, any resemblance to actual persons, living or dead, is purely coincidental. All rights reserved. No part of this book may be reproduced or transmitted in any form without written permission of the author, except by a reviewer who may quote brief passages for review purposes only.

NB: This book uses UK spelling.

MORE BOOKS BY S J CRABB

The Diary of Madison Brown

My Perfect Life at Cornish Cottage

My Christmas Boyfriend

Jetsetters

More from Life

A Special Kind of Advent

Fooling in love

Will You

Holly Island

Aunt Daisy's Letter

The Wedding at the Castle of Dreams

My Christmas Romance

Escape to Happy Ever After

Cruising in Love

Coming Home to Dream Valley

New Beginnings in Dream Valley

sjcrabb.com

CRUISING IN LOVE

Two best friends.
One broken heart.
One life-changing decision.

When Florence walked away from her wedding without her groom by her side, she thought she would never be happy again.

In a bid to put the whole experience behind her she went on honeymoon with her bridesmaid Sammy Jo.

Against her better judgement they sign up for the ship's cruising in love programme where single passengers are paired up in a bid to find their ship mate.

Seven dates in seven days with a love match at the end and another week to get to know one another.

What could possibly go wrong?

Then Florence and Sammy Jo are made an offer they should definitely refuse. Will it steer them in the wrong direction or prove to be everything they wanted in life?

A light-hearted romance about starting again and discovering that everything happens for a very good reason.

PROLOGUE

The beauty of the roses curling around the gothic arch disguise the sharp thorns hidden from view that are lying in wait to deal a sharp blow to the person who dares interfere with perfection. Guardians, soldiers, bodyguards of excellence that every rose deserves in life.

The sun casts its blistering rays through the window and causes a slight trickle of perspiration to trickle down my face. Tarnishing a different kind of perfection, one that was man made and crafted by an artist with a different kind of palette.

The man sitting beside me is my own soldier; the one responsible for defending me against harm for over twenty years already, waiting patiently to give me to another. It's not easy for him. Just the silence, the emotion that fills the small space but is so tangible it could alter destiny's trail, reminds me of that. I know he is unhappy; he doesn't need words to relay the facts, it's a silent communication between us that shows in his eyes and the tense clench of his jaw. We are quiet, both wrapped up in the scene that is unfolding outside, as we sense all is not well.

The driver makes to exit the car and my father says tersely, "Can you give us a minute?"

"Of course, sir."

He steps outside respectfully, giving us the desired privacy and my heart races as I sense fate watching with interest.

"Something isn't right."

My father speaks in a voice laced with tension and I see the anxious expression on my mum's face as she hovers near the entrance to the church, trying to look busy as she fusses with the bridesmaid's dresses, flowers - anything to disguise the anxiety she is feeling right now.

The vicar is also looking at his watch and stealing nervous glances towards the vintage white Rolls Royce that is waiting patiently outside.

He's not here.

I can feel it in the depths of my soul. Oliver isn't here. Don't ask me how I know, I just do and my father takes my hand and squeezes it, before saying softly, "Shall I have a word?"

I nod, biting my lower lip as I watch a scene unfold I'm strangely detached from.

My father exits the car and approaches the group and steers my mum away to the side as she whispers in his ear.

Part of me wonders if anyone from Oliver's family is even present because there's an eerie sense of calm settled over the church, an emptiness, an unopened gift with nothing inside.

My father turns and I feel their stares piercing my heart with pity. My fingers tangle in my lap and I find them strangely fascinating as my heart starts thumping as it senses an approaching storm.

Thinking back to the strange call I received back at the house, it all slots into place.

"Remember I'll always love you, Florrie."

His voice sounded hesitant, scared even, and I put it down to nerves. Six words were all he said before he cut the call and far from filling me with confidence, they felt a lot like goodbye even then.

Maybe it's been the growing sense of distance between us that has increased over the months since we started planning the wedding. His lack of interest in the details. The acceptance of a situation we both said we wanted. The endless planning meetings and arguments over the colour of the bridesmaid's dresses and type of flowers to grace the tables, along with the order of service and hymns chosen. There was the important decision of what gifts to buy for our wedding party and the choice of venue to hold it.

This wedding has been months, if not years of planning and somewhere along the way we lost all enthusiasm for it. For each other actually because I'm guessing that Oliver has done what I was too much of a coward to do – stopped this train before it crashed.

My father starts walking slowly back to me and I know from his face my fears are correct. There will be no wedding today, no happily ever after for Oliver Hunter-Smythe and Florence Monroe. No house in the country and honeymoon on a Caribbean cruise. No life together and no creating of lives. It's over before it even began and strangely, I'm more than happy about that.

Looking past my father, I see the stricken expression on my mother's face as she talks earnestly to the waiting vicar. My best friend Sammy Jo looks around in confusion and my friends Stephanie and Molly stand checking their phones. As my father opens the door, I inhale sharply and hold my breath for the truth.

"I'm sorry, Florrie."

He looks devastated, destroyed and yet it's outlined in relief. It hurts him deeply to think of me upset in any way and yet how can I tell him how happy I am right now. Oliver has set me free; I owe him that at least and so I nod and say softly, "It's fine dad, you don't need to explain."

He looks surprised and I smile sadly. "I had a feeling this was going to happen. Maybe you should just head inside and cancel the wedding. Send the guests home and tell them how sorry we are to drag them here unnecessarily."

He looks confused and shakes his head.

"What are you talking about, darling, everyone is waiting inside and has been for some time?"

"Oliver?" I look up in surprise as his jaw clenches and he looks so angry it makes my heart beat just a little faster. "He's there - barely."

"What do you mean, for goodness' sake dad, please just tell me?"

"He's a little off his head to put it mildly. Your mum thinks he's drunk but isn't ruling out drugs. He can barely string a sentence together and is being inappropriate with one of the guests."

"In what way – inappropriate?"

He sighs heavily and almost spits, "With a woman sitting on his side of the church. I think the term they use is snogging these days but I'm so old it's probably a different one now."

"What woman?"

Dad looks uncomfortable. "Your mum says she doesn't

know who she is but looks like the sort of girl with loose morals and no fashion sense. Her words not mine."

For a second, I'm horrified, angry and insulted. My groom is snogging someone in the congregation in front of our families and friends minutes before I walk down the aisle dressed like a toilet roll holder.

Something happens in a split second that changes everything. It's as if the world shifts and I tumble sideways and as it rights itself, I am set on a different path. The future looks different somehow, clearer, brighter even, and a strange sense of calm settles around me like a halo.

Smiling, I look at my dad and say softly, "Shall we?"

He looks confused as I edge to the door and open it, allowing the soft breeze to ruffle the silk on my ultra-long dress and take deep breaths of the holy air that surrounds this place of worship.

I stand and a photographer appears out of nowhere and starts issuing orders and through it all I smile and act as if I haven't got a care in the world.

My father looks a little confused as I hold out my arm. "We should get inside; I am getting married after all."

"But…"

He falters, and I shake my head. "We're doing this, dad. I'm not going to let anything ruin this day for me because I have waited my whole life for this moment and nothing you say will change my mind."

He looks upset, angry even, and I try not to look at the disappointment in his eyes.

As we approach the group waiting for us patiently, I smile and my mum shares a look with my dad of confusion and alarm.

"Florrie…"

"Go inside, mum, we can't keep them waiting any longer."

She throws an agonising look to my father but as my bridesmaids crowd around me she has no choice but to step inside.

The vicar looks worried and makes to speak and I fix him with a blinding smile and say with determination. "I'm ready."

He follows my mother and as my father takes my arm, I whisper, "Trust me dad."

He nods but looks crushed, as if he's leading me to the gallows, and as the music starts, I set my resolve in place.

This is it. Months of planning, vast expense and sleepless nights follow me inside as we start the short walk down the aisle to the rest of my life.

As we walk, I feel the pity reach out and punch me hard in the face. The guests are standing, but nobody holds my gaze. They look worried, uncomfortable and are probably wondering if they should speak up at the point in the service when the vicar asks if anyone objects to the wedding taking place. Just imagining the chorus of objections when asked would be music to my ears, but they aren't likely to offer them.

Now everyone in this church knows this is a bad idea, which is something I've known for quite some time now, and I hate myself for allowing it to get this far in the first place.

I look with interest at Oliver's side of the church, wondering which of these women has just shared saliva with my fiancé. It soon becomes obvious when I see a rather rough looking woman wearing a body-con dress with her red lipstick smeared across her lips, throwing daggers in my general direction. For a moment I'm confused because this woman looks as if she charges by the hour. Maybe she does and Oliver hired her to give me reason to call the whole thing off.

My heart hardens when I see my grandmother openly weeping when she catches sight of me approaching. My aunts, uncles, cousins and friends are looking sick as they throw me worried looks and daggers in Oliver's direction. His own family looks uncomfortable and I'm a little entertained by that. I know they never thought I was good enough for Oliver. Born into wealth and high society, his future was mapped out from the cradle. Public school, Eton and then a position in his father's law firm. Yes, we had it all it seemed, when in reality we had nothing worth keeping anyway.

As I draw near to the man himself, I see the bloodshot eyes of a man in purgatory. He looks dishevelled, as if he's been in a fight, and I glance at his best man who is clenching his fist angrily beside him. He looks at me apologetically and I smile at him with a happiness I shouldn't be experiencing right now.

Then I smile at Oliver and take his sweaty hand as the music stops and the vicar clears his throat.

Before he can speak, I hold up my hand and clasping Oliver's tightly, I turn to face the congregation.

"Ladies and gentlemen, friends, family and hangers on."

I look at the woman as I say it and see the understanding in her eyes.

"And Oliver, my poor foolish groom who, as it turns out, just isn't worth keeping."

There's a shocked intake of breath as I turn and face him and stroke his face softly before saying sadly, "I'm setting you free, Oliver. You don't want this; I don't want this and my family certainly doesn't want this. I deserve better than you, so have a nice life, consider yourself dumped at the altar and I'm guessing there isn't a person here who disagrees. So, just in case you haven't understood me correctly, I no longer want to marry you and probably never did. Goodbye Oliver, please be happy because despite everything I want that for you."

"Florrie."

His voice sounds broken yet edged in relief, and he stumbles a little towards me. "I'm… well, I'm sorry."

"Leaning forward, I brush my lips against his face and whisper, "I forgive you and just for the record, always remember I loved you too. It's why I'm doing this; we both deserve better."

Pressing my lips to his forehead, I take one last look at the man who has made me stronger and as I walk away, it's with a new spring to my step and hope in my heart. I'll be ok. More than ok and now it's time to spread my wings and fly.

1

The bed dips and I almost spill the champagne all over the pristine Egyptian cotton sheets. "Careful, Sammy Jo, we've got to sleep in here tonight."

She giggles and thumps the goose feather pillow with earnest. "At least you'll get some sleep, you wouldn't if things had worked out differently."

"If you are referring to my wedding night, you are probably right. Mind you, Oliver could hardly stand, let alone, well, you know."

"You can say the word, Florrie."

"No, I can't."

I laugh as she rolls her eyes. "You're such a prude."

"One of us has to be."

She clinks glasses with me and we settle back against the sumptuous pillows and pass the silver platter of strawberries dipped in chocolate between us. "So, this is unexpected. Are you sure you're ok with this?"

"Of course. I keep on telling anyone who will listen that if I feel anything it's relief."

"Your parents looked worried, though. Mind you, they

also looked so relieved it made me question whether they wanted you to marry Oliver in the first place."

"I think they did at first but as time went on, even they began to see we weren't suited."

Sammy Jo turns and says with interest, "Why did you let it get this far, then? You should have pulled out months ago."

"I'm not sure." I shrug and sigh heavily. "It just seemed easier to go with it and I suppose I didn't want to upset anyone."

"Yes, I can see how much better it was to wait until the very last minute before detonating the bomb that blew your worlds apart."

She rolls her eyes and grabs another strawberry. "If it's any consolation, I think you did the right thing. Oliver was never good enough for you. Any man with floppy hair and a wandering eye deserves all he gets."

"Maybe, although I felt a little sorry for him if I'm honest."

Just thinking of the fallout he was left to deal with as I drove away from the chaos makes me feel a little bad, but then again, he could have stopped this at any time if he was having doubts.

"You know, Sammy, it's taught me one thing, don't live your life to please others. If I had been truthful to myself, I would never have agreed to marry him in the first place."

"Then why did you?"

"Because I thought he was what I wanted – the life I wanted. You know, successful husband, a country house, two kids and a range rover with a couple of black Labradors. I was sold on that idea from an early age, but when it came to it, it felt as if I was about to step out of that church into middle age. It felt so final, like the gates were closing and locked behind me. I haven't lived, not really. Why was I so keen to grow up and become an adult when I haven't started living yet?"

"I know what you mean." Sammy Jo sucks the strawberry noisily and dips it in her champagne before going in for a second round.

"I made a vow to travel the world and have experiences before I settle for normal."

"Since when?" I stare at her incredulously, and she laughs. "Since I watched Jane McDonald on that cruise programme. You know, that woman is living her best life. She gets paid to sail around the world in luxury and has experiences many of us only have once in a lifetime. I want that. Extreme living, I call it and if I can just find a way to be her replacement, I will set sail and never look back."

"Then why don't we?"

"Explain." She looks at me sharply, and I grin.

"I happen to know of a cruise leaving in just two days' time with a spare cabin and my name on one of the tickets. I'm pretty certain we can transfer Oliver's to you and we could enjoy two weeks sailing around the Caribbean while we work out our next step."

"Are you serious?" Sammy jumps up, her eyes shining. "Really."

Laughing, I grab the champagne and fill our glasses.

"Yes, let's do this. We'll be like Thelma and Louise, the seafaring versions. We will have adventures and conquer new continents."

"But how, what will I tell my manager?"

"Tell him you quit."

I start to laugh as she stares at me in horror. "Quit, are you mad? Why would I quit the production line in Hainsey's electromagnet components? I'm living the dream."

"You know you're only there until something better comes along and it has. My honeymoon. Let's do this, Sammy Jo. Let's take off on an all-expenses paid holiday and see where it takes us. You'll find a job when we get back, if not I'll hire you myself. Come on, let's do this and show everyone we are indestructible."

"Ok." Her eyes shine as she jumps up and hugs me so tightly I almost spill the contents of the glass. "Of course I will. I'd be a fool to turn this one down."

For a moment we grin stupidly at one another as we contemplate a moment of madness borne out of devastation. We are no longer thinking straight and have officially lost our minds, which is the best possible state to be in to force change.

As we clink glasses in the honeymoon suite of the Astoria Plaza, it's with the realisation that we will wake up to a different future in the morning than the one that was waiting for us.

2

The Aphrodite is magnificent. We stand waiting our turn to board and are stunned into silence. After what has been the most emotional two days of my life, I can't believe that we are really doing this. Sammy Jo has gone all in for this and quit her job and now the champagne effect has worn off, I'm feeling decidedly responsible for that decision.

"Wow, I never believed it would be so huge."

"That's what all the girls say, darlin'."

We spin around and see two men leering at us a little too close for comfort and I'm shocked when Sammy Jo winks at them before turning back to me and whispering, "Wow, we've pulled already, I knew this was a good idea."

"What are you talking about, have you seen how old they are?"

I stare at her in horror and she giggles. "So what, if they are fun and good company I may be persuaded to lower my expectations."

I daren't look around because the last thing I need is another man in my life.

Pulling her with me as the line shifts, I say with a warning, "Strictly no men. Not for the next two weeks, if not ever. I need to detox, de-cleanse and destress and no man is about to complicate my life anytime soon."

"Spoilsport." She giggles and I roll my eyes as we inch further up the line.

"Mind you..." She leans in and lowers her voice. "I feel a little out of it if you know what I mean."

"No, I don't."

"Have you seen the age of these people? I think we're the youngest ones here."

"In our line maybe, but there are thousands more people on board and I'm pretty sure many will be our age. Anyway, it doesn't matter, we aren't here to make friends, we're here for the adventure."

She nods and snaps a photo on her phone. "For my Instagram."

She pulls me close and takes a selfie of us and for a moment I forget who should have been beside me. This is exciting, unknown and a little bit scary and it feels so good to be leaving all the emotional baggage behind.

Luckily, my parents took charge and kept me away from the fallout I created, and Sammy Jo has kept me company ever since. The next day we packed to fly to Fort Lauderdale and here we are, boarding my honeymoon cruise.

As we inch further up the gangplank she says with interest, "Does Oliver know we're going?"

Thinking of my jilted groom I feel a tiny pang of regret and say sadly, "I don't know. Because the booking was made by my dad, I'm not sure if he needed Oliver's permission to change the name on the tickets."

"Do you think he would be angry if he knew we were here?"

Cruising in Love

"No, my father paid so he has no claim to it."

"Is your dad ok with this? He could have taken your mum for a much-needed stress relief break."

Thinking of my parents, I smile softly. "He wanted us to go. Said we needed it and just enjoy ourselves."

"Then we will. It would be rude not to after they have gone to all this trouble."

Once again, we pose for the camera as the ship's photographer records the momentous occasion when we step onto the ship and as we move away, we stare around in astonishment.

"Wow." Sammy Jo says in awe, and I'm much the same. As floating hotels go, this one is extremely decadent and I stare in wonder at the huge reception area.

"It's just like a posh hotel." Sammy gasps as we stare at the deep plush carpeting and mirrored walls. A fountain takes centre stage and all around us is the buzz of conversation as excited travellers check in to paradise.

We wait our turn, and I look around in excitement. Two weeks of luxury beckon and I am so ready for this.

We take up our position behind a couple who look as if they do this all the time, and I listen to their conversation with interest. "It's not as nice as the Princess Sophia."

"Nothing ever is." Her husband grumbles beside her as she stares around her with a hint of distaste. "You did book us a cabin near the main deck. I hate being deep inside the bowels."

"You know I did, stop moaning."

"Gloria Munday came on this cruise last year and said she got food poisoning; do you think we'll be that unlucky?"

Her husband shakes his head and groans. "For god's sake, woman, this cruise cost a small fortune and you will enjoy every minute of it, or I'll..."

Sammy giggles and nudges me. "What's the chance he'll toss her overboard inside the hour."

The woman turns around and glares at us, and Sammy tries desperately to stop giggling as I turn away. Luckily, we are directed to another line and I whisper, "I hope we don't end up next to them at dinner because she'll poison our food after that comment."

Sammy just shrugs. "Somebody needs to tell her. I mean, how can anyone complain, this place is five star all the way."

I must agree with her because I don't think I've even seen such luxury and I've been to every country hotel with Oliver within one hundred miles on getaways.

However, this is in a different league entirely and I feel a little guilty at how happy I'm feeling when I should be devastated at the mess my life is in right now.

"Good morning ladies."

One of the staff greets us and smiles warmly. "Welcome on board the Aphrodite. Have you checked in and received your key card already?"

I nod because we have already passed through all the stringent security measures and check in procedure before we even set foot on board and she smiles.

"Your stateroom is ready and you can either proceed straight there or take time to explore on the way. You should have a map of the ship in your welcome pack, along with instructions. If you like, you can grab a bite to eat in the buffet restaurant, it's open for snacks and welcome drinks. Do you have any questions?"

She is already looking past us to the next in line, so I say quickly, "No thank you."

It feels as if we have been given our freedom to explore,

so without any further delay, we set off to see what the Aphrodite has to offer.

As we wander around, we take many selfies and try to absorb the place we will call home for the next two weeks.

"Can you believe this, Florrie, it's like another world?"

Sammy's eyes are huge as she stares around in awe, and I have to agree with her.

"There's even a shopping mall here, Sammy, I am now officially in heaven."

I blink in surprise because we have stepped into Narnia because all around us are individual shops selling exciting things and in the centre are escalators powering up many levels in an apparent endless number of floors. The sheer scale of this operation overwhelms me a little, and it's almost too much to take in.

As well as the shopping mall, we see signs for the theatre, casino, spa and gym. Nothing has been left to chance and a whole new world is opening up to me and it feels amazing.

In a daze we wander around and I don't think I'll ever find my way to my stateroom but against all the odds it's not long before we discover what will be our home for the next two weeks.

3

Sammy actually squeals when she sees the luxury waiting for us as I blink in shock.

"I love your parents." She flies around the room like a banshee, opening cupboards, jumping on the bed and generally shrieking at the top of her voice as we take in the luxury waiting for us.

As cabins go, this one is beautiful. Decorated in blue and white florals, the huge bed looks out towards double sliding doors that lead to a balcony overlooking the ocean. To one side behind a partition wall is a huge walk-in shower and his and hers vanity units. There is even some kind of towel origami going on as we stare at a couple of swan towels resplendent on the side and the array of posh lotions and potions that greet us is every woman's delight.

There is a beautifully wrapped fruit basket nestling beside a magnum of champagne, with a small box of truffles set to the side.

"Oh yes, this will do nicely." Sammy Jo claps her hands and pulls open the doors and we step outside and stare in amazement at the view of the ocean that beckons us to experience more adventures than we can surely stand.

A knock on the door interrupts us and I head inside and open it, revealing a porter delivering our luggage.

"I'm sorry this is late, ma'am. Please accept our apologies."

"It's fine, thank you, we've just arrived."

As the porter wheels it in, Sammy appears and stares at the man with obvious interest and I shake my head as she says huskily, "Thank you so much, um, Tony." She reads his name badge as she flutters her eyelashes and he grins in a lopsided, cheeky, player kind of way. "My pleasure."

The word rolls off his tongue with practised ease and she blushes a little and says slightly breathlessly, "I'm Sammy Jo and this is my friend, Florrie. I feel a little cheeky asking but we're new to cruising, so I may annoy you with questions."

He smiles, and I see a twinkle in his eye as he grins. "I'm at your service, night or day."

He winks, and she blushes a little and I just stare at her in shock. What's going on? We're not even unpacked for goodness's sake, and this is the second man she's made eyes at. Admittedly, he's a huge improvement on the first but really!

"So, Tony, how does one go about getting a job on a cruise liner?"

She smiles at him coyly, and I feel like the third wheel as he inches a little closer to her. "It depends what your talents are?"

She grins and flutters her eyelashes – again. "I can turn my hand to most things."

"Sounds good."

He appears in no hurry to leave and Sammy says with a

giggle, "Maybe we could discuss any opportunities when you finish work, if that's ok with you, of course."

"I'm sure that could be arranged."

They are now openly staring at one another and any oxygen in this cabin has been eradicated because I'm almost chocking on the fumes of being extremely cringed out.

Tony appears to remember he's actually working and says quickly, "I'll look forward to catching up later then."

"Me too."

As he backs out of the room, I stare at her with raised eyes and as the door closes, she sighs. "Wow, I knew this was a good idea. He's perfect."

"Sammy Jo Miles, you haven't even unpacked yet and have propositioned the porter. What's the matter with you, you're out of control?"

To my surprise, Sammy sighs and sits on the edge of the bed, and looks a little wistful.

"I'm sorry, Florrie, it's not been that easy for me lately."

"Why, you never said?"

I perch beside her and she pulls a face. "It's easy for you. Oliver was in your life as soon as you finished school, and I was always a little envious of what you had. Nobody ever looked at me the way he looked at you and I was a little jealous if I'm honest."

"You never said."

I feel bad because I never even considered Sammy was struggling, and she shakes her head. "Even though I've tried – rather hard as it happens, I've never had any success attracting the right kind of man. You know, the keeper as opposed to the heartbreaker. Seeing you find Oliver and move on with your life just highlighted my own lack of judgement and poor decisions. I decided that I would let no opportunity pass by and have made it my goal to find a husband by the end of the year before I reconsider my life choices.

"Life choices, what are you talking about?" I am feeling a little confused because surely it's not that urgent. I mean, we are only twenty-three years old and hardly spinsters. I can't see what the urgency is.

"Well..." Sammy sighs. "I have decided to manifest my life. You know, believe that I can do anything and think it's really happening. By my reckoning, if it works, I should be married by the end of the year, or at least engaged and living in Florida."

"Wait, what? Since when did you want to live in Florida?"

"Since I watched a programme on it. I mean, quite honestly Florrie, why live anywhere else? Wall to wall sunshine, gorgeous guys, an outdoors kind of life and Disney World. They really are living the dream."

"Sammy Jo..." I shake my head. "Maybe you are overthinking this, um, manifestation thing. I mean, you are still young, there really is no hurry and I am now in the same position as you, despite having supposedly found my 'one.' My experience teaches us that you need to wait for the right man to come along. You can't force the issue because it will ultimately fail. If I were you and I am now, actually, you should take a step back, be happy within yourself first before you start looking for someone to share it all with."

I squeeze her hand reassuringly. "Listen, we haven't even unpacked yet and you are lining up potential husbands. Let's just take a breath and forget about men for the next two weeks at least. Unwind, de-stress and enjoy this amazing opportunity. Grab a suntan, broaden our horizons and eat more food that we can cope with. Then and only then, when we wave goodbye to the sea, will we look to the future and decide where to go from here. Deal?"

She looks undecided and yet nods. "Ok, that sounds like a plan."

Glancing down, I see her fingers crossed behind her back and sigh inside. Sammy Jo appears to be on a mission and it will take all my energy to stop her on her quest. The only thing I can do is manage her somehow, which is most annoying because if I know my friend, she will have husband number one lined up by dinner tomorrow evening.

4

I'm not sure how we ended up here but I feel strangely at home in a life jacket.

Sammy giggles. "I'm not sure if yellow is my colour. I wish they did them in pink and pale blue."

She twirls in front of me as we stand at our muster station, as instructed by the staff. Apparently, this is the drill we need to master before we even set sail and it feels strange mingling with the crowd as we all learn what to do in an emergency.

"This is so tedious, Geoffrey."

A woman grumbles beside me and Sammy nudges me sharply and whispers, "I think this is fun. Imagine if we really did have to abandon ship. We may even get winched on board a rescue helicopter by a navy SEAL, how romantic."

"There's nothing romantic about this at all. If you ask me, the sooner this ordeal is over the better. Anyway, we are off men, remember."

The woman beside us looks over sharply and shakes her head. "Off men girls, at your age. I don't think so."

She shifts closer and rakes us over with her imperial gaze. "Two attractive women like you shouldn't be off men already. Especially on board a ship named after the goddess of love."

Sammy nods. "Tell me about it. I keep on trying to explain to my friend that this is the perfect opportunity to find love."

The woman nods vigorously. "I agree." She smiles and waves towards her companion, a rather portly man who looks a little ridiculous in a lifejacket that appears a few sizes too small. "I met Geoffrey on the Princess Allegra, five years ago. My second husband had died a few weeks before, and I was mourning him at the time."

"Wow, second husband, you obviously know your stuff." Sammy looks at the woman as if she's about to reveal the secrets of the universe and the woman nods majestically. "I think formal introductions are needed before we proceed. My name is Ellen Winter and my husband is Geoffrey Winter, retired insurance broker from Tunbridge Wells. This is our seventh cruise together, but my tally is far greater than that. I have met all my husbands on cruise ships and let me tell you, there is not a better place in my opinion to weed out the wheat from the chaff."

Sammy's eyes are huge as she hangs onto the woman's every word, but my heart is sinking as fast as this ship would if it hit an iceberg in the Antarctic.

"So, here's the plan." Ellen leans closer and looks around furtively, as if she's planning a covert operation. "You must both sign up to the ship's cruising in love programme."

"The what?" I can't believe I'm hearing this and Sammy says excitedly, "Yes, what's that all about?"

"They are running a club to encourage the single passengers to mingle. I signed up for a similar programme on the cruise where I met Geoffrey. It encourages people to socialise and adds a little excitement to the cruise. I can't recommend it highly enough, it certainly worked for me and I had a lot of fun in the process."

"What does it involve?" I feel a little dubious about what sounds like speed dating at sea and Ellen says wistfully, "You sign up and are assigned your match every day for seven days. By the end of the week, you have dated seven suitably matched partners based on the preferences you set at the beginning of the cruise. The second week is all about spending time with the person you matched with and seeing if you are the perfect fit. I must say, I'm almost envious because I had so much fun when it was my time. You really should consider it. It will certainly make the cruise more interesting."

Sammy nods vigorously. "Where do I sign up?"

"Um, Sammy, remember our conversation not one hour ago."

She rolls her eyes and says to Ellen, "Please excuse my friend, she's recovering from a bad experience. Me, on the other hand, I have no experience at all so this is right up my street."

Ellen looks at me and sighs. "Ah, a broken heart, I've had many of those."

She fixes me with a sympathetic smile. "Let me tell you, young lady, the best cure for a broken heart is to plug the gap with another. Use another man to drive the images of the previous one away. You won't find I'm wrong either. In order to forget you need to focus on someone else fast. Whatever happened before was meant to, and so why waste time? Life is for living and you, my dear, have no time to waste."

Sammy nods. "She's right, Florrie, we need to sign up for

this love cruise as soon as we ditch these lifejackets. Where do we go?"

She looks at Ellen as if she knows everything and Ellen looks happy to play matchmaker. "The ship's sail away party is your best bet. Have a word with the staff on duty and they will direct you to the relevant place."

"Wow, a party – already."

Sammy is more excited than I've seen her – ever, and Ellen nods. "Yes, it's so much fun. Cocktails, music and lots of dancing. You know, cruising is so much fun and you have certainly come to the right place to forget about whatever problems you've experienced."

Geoffrey sighs heavily beside her and grumbles, "I need several cocktails to forget this tedious activity that gets more annoying every time. I am an experienced sailor; I could evacuate this ship in my sleep."

Ellen rolls her eyes. "Typical man, thinks he knows everything." She elbows him sharply. "Stop whining, Geoffrey, it's most unattractive. There's some champagne in our room. You can uncork that as soon as we get back."

He looks a little happier and as our attention is diverted to the reason we're here, the safety drill, I am left with an extremely bad feeling about this voyage of discovery because if I know my friend, she will embrace this love cruise with every ounce of enthusiasm she's got.

5

I don't think I've ever been to a party quite like this one. We haven't even left the dock, and the music is loud and the passengers out of control already. It appears that everyone is in the mood to start this holiday before we've even set sail and it's a lot to take in.

Sammy is dancing in the middle of a crowd of people while I watch from the edge of insanity, holding a brightly coloured cocktail and wondering how my life turned out this way. I should be standing beside Oliver, about to begin our voyage of self-discovery. Our lives together as husband and wife and I wonder what he would make of all this.

It was my parent's idea, a gift to the newlyweds to give them time to relax after the stresses of pledging their lives to one another.

However, this is far from relaxing and I'm guessing we would have found a quiet corner somewhere to stand hand in hand and watch the shoreline disappear from view, before taking to our cabin and doing what most people do on honeymoon.

A man nudges against me and my drink spills a little, the

brightly coloured liquid splashing onto the newly washed deck. "Sorry love."

He mumbles his apology and heads back onto the dance floor with an exuberant group of friends.

I'm a little surprised at the broad mix of people on board. There are people like Ellen and Geoffrey. Older, more seasoned travellers, who appear to do this sort of thing all the time. Then there are the rowdy groups of people who appear to be treating this as one big party already.

Couples stand on the fringes looking slightly superior about the whole thing, and families struggle to contain their children's excitement as they strain at the leash to be set free on this ship of dreams.

Edging away from the dance floor, I wander over to the rail and look at the activity on the quay. Groups of people wave frantically to loved ones who are heading off for adventure and excitement.

I feel a pang as the enormity of my situation starts to hit me. I jilted my fiancé in full view of his family, my family and God. Surely I will burn in Hell for that, but it had to be done.

It wasn't just the antics of a man who has been balancing on the edge of disaster for months now. It was a build-up of circumstances that I had been ignoring; choosing to believe that everything would work itself out in the end.

The arguments, the harsh words and disinterest in a wedding we should have been excited for, not dreading.

Oliver worked a lot and rumours of his infidelity hurt but were ignored, as I chose to believe him every time.

I wonder why he carried on with it at all. Surely if he didn't want me, he could have said. No one was forcing him – at least I don't think they were, and that is what I don't understand.

Cruising in Love

"It's all a little overwhelming, isn't it?"

A deep voice interrupts my thoughts, and I turn to see a man leaning on the rail beside me. He must be in his early thirties with dark hair and the look of a man who has life all worked out. His clothes are designer; I recognise the brand logo on his jacket and the chinos he's wearing are crease free and look well made. His sunglasses are an expensive brand and he looks as if he runs a multi-billion-pound company – for fun.

"It is." I smile and look with curiosity at the stranger beside me who has the deepest blue twinkling eyes and a kind smile and I note the tanned strong forearms of a man who probably enjoys hot foreign holidays more frequently than most.

"Is this your first time?"

He arches his brow and for some reason, the look he washes over me makes me feel a little uncomfortable. It's the kind of look that sees inside your mind, and I shiver a little as his eyes strip me of any hiding place; as if he knows every thought in my head and those I have yet to work out.

"Yes." My mouth is dry and I lick my lips as he shifts a little closer and whispers, "I thought so."

Turning, I look at the crowd on the quayside and say softly, "It's organised chaos and a little overwhelming if I'm honest."

He leans on the rail and says with a husky drawl, "I love this part of the cruise the most. The anticipation, the sense of adventure, the thought that anything can happen, stretching out before me like a book waiting to be written."

"What do you do – for a living I mean?"

I'm curious because if I had to guess I would have him down as a banker or business man."

"I run my own property company."

"That sounds interesting."

"It is – very. I sell houses; a virtual estate agent with an extremely tangible product."

"How does that work?"

I find myself relaxing as the ship starts to glide gracefully out of the harbour, and even the loud music fades a little into the background as I listen with interest to a stranger.

"I sell houses online and use videos to show them off. Mainly I use glamorous women to demonstrate the property and offer a virtual experience that can be viewed anywhere in the world."

"That sounds interesting. Do you sell many houses that way?"

"More than you think. The market is hungry and I am feeding it well."

He smiles and looks interested. "What about you..."

"Florence." I smile shyly and he returns it with a pleasant, "I'm Marcus, pleased to meet you."

"Well..." I laugh, slightly nervously. "I'm here on my honeymoon with my bridesmaid, actually."

"Interesting." He grins, showing a perfect set of Simon Cowell teeth and I nod. "My husband to be never made the grade and so here we are, enjoying what should have been our honeymoon because it would be a shame to waste it."

He looks a little concerned, and I shrug. "It's all a bit sad when you think about it."

"Are you – sad I mean because you don't look it, if you don't mind me saying?"

"No, I'm not."

I lean with my back against the rail and watch the crowd partying hard before me. "I'm relieved more than anything.

Oliver wasn't the man for me, I knew that months ago; in fact, I think I've always known that."

"Then why did you agree to marry him?"

Marcus turns to look at me, and I feel slightly foolish that I let it get so far.

"It was just easier to go along with it."

The ship's horn sounds, making us both jump and Marcus laughs softly. "It appears that our voyage is officially underway."

"It does." I sip my cocktail and look at him from under my lashes and surprise myself that I'm enjoying his company. He has an easy way about him that makes me feel comfortable and not threatened and yet before I can say anything else he stands and says pleasantly, "Well, it was nice to meet you, Florence. I hope you enjoy your cruise with your bridesmaid."

I nod, feeling a little disappointed that he's leaving already, and he smiles. "I should go and unpack, work a little, you know the routine."

"Of course, I should really go and find my friend, anyway."

For some reason I feel a little shy around him and he appears to hesitate for a moment and then leans in and whispers in my ear, "If it helps, I think you did the right thing. If something's not right, correct it. Move on and take the lesson you learned with you. Don't make the same mistake again because you are too important for that. Do what makes Florence happy, you owe it to yourself."

He straightens up and I say almost desperately, "Are you?"

"Happy?"

I nod as he runs that lazy gaze across me like a warm Summer breeze.

"I make it my business to be happy, Florence, because why waste a minute of the rest of your life. My dreams have been methodically planned to allow me to live it in the best way possible, so word of advice, set your goals, make them happen, and then set them again. Keep on setting them and never settle because the world is yours if you reach out and take it."

"Florrie."

I hear Sammy approaching, screaming my name above the loud music, and I turn to wave at her. As she finds me in the crowd and makes her way towards me, I am disappointed when I turn back to find that Marcus has gone already. Why am I disappointed and what was it about him that makes me search for him in the crowd? That's exactly what I'm doing now with the desperation of a woman who wants to learn more about the man who appeared out of nowhere and spoke a lot of sense – to me, anyway.

6

Sammy Jo is deep in thought as she stares at the screen. We are in our stateroom and I'm currently unpacking as she contemplates the form required to enter the Cruising in love programme.

"What am I looking for exactly and how can I word, tall, dark, handsome and rich without appearing narcissistic and flaky?"

"Why not, it's like a wish list to Santa because it's doubtful such a man exists, anyway."

"There speaks the voice of disappointment."

I sigh and sit beside her on the bed and look at the television screen that is doubling as some kind of computer.

"Do you blame me? I mean, I have been let down by a tall, dark and handsome man who turned out to be a tall, dark and cheating man, making me wonder if there is anyone decent out there at all."

"He's on this ship, I just know it."

She screws up her face in concentration and says slowly, "Somewhere on this ship is my future husband. I can feel it, don't ask me how, I just do."

"You feel nothing, just hope."

"You may not believe me, but I do. Call it a premonition, but as soon as I stepped on board this vessel, I knew he was here. Destiny is calling, and it has a big, fat, red ribbon tied around it. You know, Florrie, I don't think it was coincidental that you jilted Oliver at the altar and dragged me on this honeymoon in his place. It was always going to happen and what led us here was fate."

"Then fate has a warped sense of humour. Couldn't she have left out the part where I crushed souls in the process?"

"Oh, he'll get over it, in fact he probably already has."

"I'm not talking about Oliver's."

The tears prick behind my eyes and Sammy turns to look at me with concern. "Hey, don't cry."

She wraps her arm around me and for some reason I can't stop the emotion from spilling over the edge, as the tears run down my face in remembrance of a life I should be starting right now.

"Why did I let it get so far, Sammy? Why wasn't I strong enough?"

"Because."

"What?"

"Because you thought it was what you wanted. You got swept up in the dream the world tells you from an early age you want. To meet someone, fall in love, get married and share that life together before breeding the next generation and telling them they want it too."

"Are you saying that's wrong? I mean, isn't that exactly what you're striving for yourself because you're the one filling out a form to meet the man of your dreams?"

"True, but that's because I want that life. I want the husband, kids and life by numbers. It doesn't mean it has to be that way. Maybe you're wired differently. Perhaps you want more than that and fate has stopped you before you make a big mistake."

"Thankfully."

I smile through my tears and Sammy says quickly, "Why don't you fill out the form, too? Not for the same reason as me, but to live a little. Enjoy a few dates and test your heart out. See if it's what you really want or maybe something else. You may not be ready to share your life with a man and need to find Florence Monroe first. Don't waste this opportunity and embrace it hard."

"Since when did you become so wise, Sammy?"

Shaking my head, I grin as she shrugs. "I've always been wise, disguised in stupidity. It's what makes me so mysterious and interesting."

"If you say so."

Rolling my eyes, I turn my attention to the screen and read what she's already written.

"Mountain climbing – since when?"

I stare at her list of interests with horror when I notice she has listed just about everything she has never done in her life before.

"I went climbing on that kid's wall at Brockett's farm once."

"And kayaking, since when?"

"I watched a guy I was dating do it once. From the shore actually but it still counts."

I start to giggle as I snort, "A love of poetry, since when?"

"Since I was given a book on it one Christmas."

"That you received when you were five. Honestly, Sammy, who is this person on the screen; you're not being honest?"

"Listen, this is my one shot at ordering my perfect man, and if I have to bend the rules a little, I will. Nobody wants to meet a girl from Leatherhead who is only interested in beer pong and shopping. They also want the dream and I am not denying them that pleasure. I'm guessing most of the entries will be fabricated anyway, so I'm just playing the game."

"Good for you."

We share a look and if there was any other person I could choose in the world to be here right now, it's the girl who always has been. My unofficial sister and the woman who has been by my side since we sat together in primary school. Slightly mad, desperate even, but with a heart of gold who would be the perfect match for any deserving man. So, I smile softly, "You be whoever you want to be and show them how fantastic you are. Any man would be lucky to spend time with you Sammy Jo Miles, you are amazing."

"I know."

She grins and turns back to the screen, saying lightly, "You are too, remember. Don't hold back, Florrie and seize the day and take what life offers because knowing you, destiny packed herself in your suitcase and is banging on the lid to get out. Don't let what happened with Oliver stop you. It happened, move on and this time sprint to the finish because I'm running already and you need to catch me up."

With a few clicks, she turns and looks at me triumphantly. "There, one application signed and sealed. Now we wait for destiny to come calling."

"Good for you. This will be interesting to watch if nothing else. Let the games begin."

Handing her a glass of champagne, we clink glasses and for some reason my thoughts turn to Marcus and I wonder if he has anything to do with mine. Meeting him was unexpected, strange even, but there was something about him that interested me. The trouble is, this ship is bigger than a small town and it will be a miracle if our paths cross again, anyway.

7

Our first evening is spent exploring the ship and the most interesting part was when we discovered the gallery of photographs taken of the passengers as they embarked this morning.

"Have you found us yet?"

Sammy is scrutinising every face and I shake my head. "Not yet, but there are a lot to sift through."

"I like the look of this one. Do you think he's on the cruising in love programme?"

Peering closer, I see a rather attractive man smouldering into the camera. "Maybe, he's dark and handsome, could be tall, then again, I'm guessing most people list that as a requirement, it's pretty standard."

"Maybe, but I'm not just settling for anyone you know. This is a serious quest to find my one true love."

"Good luck with that."

I move onto the next wall and find myself looking for Marcus. It annoys me that I've fixated on him already when men are the last thing on my agenda right now. I'm not sure why he interests me, maybe because I'm feeling a little vulnerable right now, but there was something intriguing about him.

"Here's Ellen and Geoffrey."

I crowd around Sammy and note Ellen's rather smug smile as Geoffrey looks irritated at being made to pose. "Do you think we'll be on their table at dinner?" Sammy sounds hopeful and I shrug. "I hope not. To be honest, I don't want to be at anyone's table at dinner. The last thing I want to make is small talk."

"But what if they are a couple of hot single billionaires on the lookout for love? It could happen you know."

Sammy sounds wistful and I say abruptly, "In your dreams."

We carry on looking and after a while Sammy groans. "I'm starving. Shall we head off to dinner?"

"Sounds good, now you mention it I can't remember the last meal I had."

We leave the gallery and head off to the main dining room and once again I wonder how different my experience would have been if I were here with Oliver. I don't miss the couples everywhere, lovingly holding hands and it makes my heart bleed when I think of what happened just two days ago.

We are shown to a table in the centre of the room and after ordering some drinks are left to wander the buffet that is set out in all its glory.

"Wow, we won't starve on this voyage that's for sure." Sammy grabs a plate and starts piling it with all sorts of delicious looking food and I soon join in. By the time we have overloaded our plates and taken our seats, I feel a lot better about this trip and feel myself finally relaxing.

Luckily, we appear to be seated on a table for six and are the only ones here at the moment and as we eat, Sammy looks at me with concern.

"How are you feeling now the dust has settled and you've had time to think?"

I shrug and spear a bite of smoked salmon and sigh. "The most surprising thing of all is that I don't miss him. I thought that once my initial anger had died down, I would regret my decision."

"I wondered if you would."

"Do you think I made the wrong call; what would you have done?"

Sammy shrugs. "Probably the same, but I would have punched him and the girl before I left."

"No you wouldn't." I laugh as she nods with a fierce expression. "Don't get me wrong, Florrie, you know I hate violence but to openly share saliva with an unknown woman while waiting for the love of his life doesn't make a man much of a catch in my opinion. Is it really too much to ask that the man you are about to dedicate your life to will stay away from other women forever?"

"No, it was kind of odd. Do you think he was on drugs?"

"He looked like he was, maybe someone slipped him a few and it was sabotage."

Her eyes widen and I shake my head. "I doubt that. Who would do such a thing?"

"Well..." She starts counting on her fingers. "Your dad, for one. I always got the impression he wasn't happy with your choice."

"No you didn't, since when?" I'm in shock about that because my dad has always liked Oliver and never said a bad word about him.

"I saw the looks he gave him. Torturous is the word I'd use to describe them. Then there's the best man."

"Sam!" She nods. "He's always had a thing for you. I've seen the way he steals little glances across the room, sort of wistful and unrequited."

"Now I know you're delusional."

"I know what I see. Then there's the woman in question herself. For all you know she could be his secret wife with a baby on the way and learned of your nuptials by chance one day. I'm guessing she slipped a potion in his pre-wedding cocktail and Voila, it all fell apart."

"You should write movies, Sammy, you have a very over-active imagination."

Sighing, I finish up and look around me at the tables that are filling up quickly. "Do you think I should call him?"

"And say what?"

"I don't know, ask if he's ok, find out how he's feeling."

"Do you want to?" Sammy looks at me with interest, and I nod slowly. "I think I should, it's just that this feels a little wrong. To be on my honeymoon with my bridesmaid and not the groom. Maybe I should just step outside and make the call before the main course."

Sammy rolls her eyes. "Ok, but don't blame me if you end up taking a guilt trip rather than the trip of a lifetime."

Pushing back my seat, I smile. "I won't be long."

As I weave my way through the tables, accompanied by the general buzz of conversation, I feel my heart thumping with anticipation. This is the right thing to do. To make things right and check that everything's ok. How can I possibly enjoy this trip until I have closure?

I make my way back to our stateroom because I need to be alone for this and as the silence greets me it wraps me in comfort giving me the strength to do something I should have done weeks, if not months ago – draw a line under Oliver and Florence and set us both free.

My fingers shake as I take out the phone and press the familiar entry in my contact list and I wonder if he'll even answer me. There's also a part of me that's hurt he hasn't already made the call himself.

He answers after the fourth ring and yet the voice I hear isn't his as a woman says, "Oliver's phone."

I'm taken aback a little and say quickly, "Um, is he there?"

"Sure."

I hear rustling and a whisper, "I think it's her."

He whispers something back and I can't make out the words but know it's Oliver and my heart beats furiously as I hold my breath.

"Florrie."

His voice sounds husky, and a little surprised and I say nervously, "Yes, can we talk, Oliver?"

"Sure, give me a sec."

I hear movement and more murmurings and then a door slams somewhere in the distant.

"Sorry about that, Flo, are you ok?"

"Are you?"

Something about this feels extremely off and he sighs. "I've been better but I'll live."

"Oh." I'm not sure what to say really, because he doesn't sound heartbroken at all.

"Who answered the phone?" That is the most important question in my mind right now because despite everything, I feel a little jealous thinking of another woman by his side.

There's a short pause and then he says in a low voice.

"That was Grace, my um…"

"Your what, Oliver?" I feel my voice rising and a strange

buzzing in my head that means my anxiety levels have reached code red.

"My...um, look there's no easy way to say this, Flo, but well, Grace is my wife."

"Your wife!"

The words make it out into the open and I feel a sharp pain where my heart used to be.

"Your wife." I say it again as if I need confirmation that I heard him right, and he sighs. "I should have told you months ago."

"You think?" My whole body is now shaking as I struggle to come to terms with a situation I never once saw coming. "You were married, since when?"

"Six months ago. Remember that business trip I went to in Vegas?"

I can't even speak, but he carries on anyway. "I met Grace there. She was working for the same company and we kind of clicked. Well, one thing led to another, and we tied the knot in the little white chapel and returned as husband and wife."

"I'm sorry, I'm struggling to understand."

My voice shakes as I say with disbelief, "You married a stranger while planning a wedding with me. You forgot to tell me when you returned home and carried on pretending that everything was fine. What the hell were you thinking, Oliver? Were you really going to marry me too, with wife number one in the congregation acting as a witness? There are laws against that type of thing you know."

I am stunned into silence and he says slowly, "I wanted *you* to end it, not me. It was easier that way."

"Easier." My voice is the highest it's ever been, and he says quickly, "I couldn't break up with you; I couldn't be the one to cause you pain, it needed to be you. I tried to make you call it off several times. I thought if I cooled things off, you would start to question it. But you ignored it. I tried staying away so you would become suspicious. You didn't seem to care. I tried everything to put you off me but you still wanted to go through with a wedding we both knew was doomed to fail."

"So you chose to humiliate me instead. Make me look like a fool and openly make out with one of the guests in front of my whole family. Well, way to go, Oliver, you just proved exactly why you were never good enough for me, why my parents hated you and why not one single guest at the wedding blamed me for ditching you at the altar."

"Florrie, I…"

"Save your words for someone who wants to hear them. They are formed by lies, anyway. Enjoy your marriage and your life, Oliver, because as sure as I'm counting my lucky stars I never married you, you will live unhappily ever after because any decision you make in life appears to be the wrong one."

I take a deep breath and say in a steady voice. "I'm glad I made this call because I was feeling guilty and wanted to check that you were ok. Obviously, I needn't have bothered because it appears I interrupted your wife consoling you. So, consider yourself the worst mistake I ever made and know that I am never giving you another thought. You are dead to me, Oliver and I can now move on and forget you even exist."

I cut the call before he can speak and feel the anger rising inside, consuming every part of me that ever felt sorry for him. For a moment I just sit replaying the conversation in my mind and then head out onto the balcony and stare at the dark, inky black sky littered with stars. The wind blows against my face, drying my tears and the waves offer a steady rhythm as the ship cuts through the water on a journey to a better place.

On the balcony of the ship of the goddess of love, I make a vow. I *will* move on and I *will* put myself first. Today is the start of the rest of my life and what a life that will be.

8

An eerie sense of calm accompanies me to the dining room, and Sammy looks up with concern as I approach.

"Are you ok, Flo, you've been gone ages. Did you get through to him?"

"Probably not."

I look at the plate of food before my friend and raise my eyes. "Hungry?"

She looks down and grins. "Always when the food tempts me as much as this does. You should get some."

Strangely, my appetite appears to have deserted me but I smile thinly. "Ok, I won't be a minute."

As I wander the lines looking at the amazing food on offer, it strikes me how weird this is. I should be a wreck, crying unconsolably in my stateroom, planning all sorts of unthinkable, despicable revenge on a man who has broken my heart and humiliated me in the cruellest of ways. Instead, I feel a lightness inside, free even, and that tells me that everything happened for a reason and Oliver was never the man for me.

By the time I return to my seat, another couple has joined us and I am happy about that because I don't think I'm ready to discuss the finer details of my conversation with Sammy just yet.

Instead, I look with interest at a couple who must be in their fifties looking around in awe, which tells me they must be new to this too.

The woman smiles as I sit down and Sammy says brightly, "Mandy, this is my friend Flo." She turns to me and grins. "Flo, this is Mandy and Simon. It's their first time too."

Simon nods as Mandy smiles. "It's an amazing experience already. We heard great things about cruising and it's certainly living up to expectations."

"Where are you from?"

Sammy looks interested, and Mandy smiles. "Wigan. We've lived there all our lives and always holidayed in Spain. Well, we both had a special birthday this year and decided to be bold and adventurous and do something different for a change."

"Finally." Simon rolls his eyes. "I've been nagging her for years but Mandy is a creature of habit and always wanted to return to the Solero in Magaluf every year."

"It's our home from home. Anyway, the Garcia's have always been our family from home, you never complained before."

Simon shakes his head and gazes fondly at his wife. "I have nothing to complain about."

Sammy looks at me with a soft expression and it drives another nail into my heart, because this is what I want. To find my other half, not a jagged piece that hurts when it tries to fit into place. Love shouldn't be difficult, one-sided with all the effort from one person. It should flow effortlessly and make the people happy, not anxious and despite everything part of me is glad that Oliver ripped off the band aid in the cruellest of ways because now I owe him absolutely nothing but my pity. I know it's just a matter of time before he messes up his new marriage, but I won't be around to gloat.

As Simon and Mandy head up to select their dishes, Sammy leans in and says with concern, "You were gone ages, is everything ok?"

"More than ok actually, Sammy, the call made up my mind for me."

She looks slightly anxious. "What happened?"

"I've moved on, permanently. In fact, you will be pleased to learn that I have decided to sign up for the cruising in love programme myself."

"What?" Sammy's eyes are wide as I nod with a determination that is keeping me sane right now.

"Yes, as soon as we finish, I will set my preferences and wait for the fun to begin. Let's make this a trip neither of us will ever forget."

She makes to speak but the happy couple return, making it an evening of polite small talk instead, which I'm grateful for. I need some time to process what happened before discussing it with my best friend and so I take a moment to gather my sanity around me and push what happened to the furthest reaches of my mind.

～

SAMMY LOOKS at me with horror, and I nod miserably. We made it back to our cabin and are leaning on the rail, looking into the obsidian darkness that matches my mood perfectly.

"I'm sorry, Florrie." She puts her arm around my shoulders and I sag a little.

"Thanks."

Now the news has filtered through to my soul, I am feeling a little different to earlier. The shock has worn off and been replaced with a multitude of emotions that are hard to process. I suppose the most overwhelming one is of humiliation. Oliver didn't want me – not really. He found someone better in the blink of an eye and acted foolishly and recklessly in a moment of extreme madness. I could almost forgive him if he was drunk and not of sound mind, but *six months*.

"Do you think his family knew?"

Sammy's voice shakes a little, and I know she's as shocked as I am.

"They do now, I suppose, but I'm guessing they were kept in the dark as much as I was. They aren't the kind of people who would go through with the whole debacle if they knew their son was hitched already."

"Wow, I bet he has some serious explaining to do."

"He'll manage. After all, Oliver has always got everything he wanted in life – very easily as it happened. I suppose they will be angry, shocked and disappointed but he's still their son, they'll forgive him."

"I wouldn't." Sammy's voice is tight and loaded with anger, and I smile.

"That's why I love you, Sammy Jo."

She squeezes my shoulder and as we look out at the dark, infinite expanse of water, she sighs. "Anything could happen now. Look Florrie, life is a blank canvas waiting for us to colour it in with our hopes and dreams and expectations, which I must confess, mine are extremely high."

Laughing softly, I blink away the tears and nod. "I expect nothing else, for both of us."

"So, cruising in love, that's a start at least."

"At least."

She leans on the rail and laughs softly. "This is going to be so much fun. We can compare dates and who knows, may even end up dating the same man. It could happen you know."

She breaks off and looks at me in horror. "What if we fall in love with the same man, that would be a disaster?"

"It would, then again, extremely doubtful because we have very different tastes in men."

"True, but anything could happen at sea."

"Then let the best woman win."

I laugh and she nods, once again looking out to sea. "Somewhere out there is my future – our future. Destiny is calling and I hear her cry."

"Have you been reading that poetry book again?"

Laughing, I turn and look at the bright lights of the cabin, looking like a beacon in a dark cave of despair.

"It could be worse, I suppose. At least we have options. Two whole weeks of them, actually."

"I wonder what those two weeks will bring. Hopefully two hot billionaires who are looking for love and ready to take on two crazy women with no common sense."

"I'm sure they are sharpening their chat up lines as we speak."

Sammy nods. "Come on, let's attack the mini bar. I can't believe we've left it this long."

Spying the empty bottle of champagne on the side in the room, I shake my head. Sammy's alcohol intake is only one thing I will need to control on this trip because from the look in my friend's eyes, she is set on making this trip one we will never stop talking about for the rest of our lives.

9

We wake to a new day and after breakfast head towards the Mast Bar for an informal gathering of the people who have signed up for the singles programme.

Sammy is excited and has pulled out every stop going to look amazing. "You look good, Sammy, any one of these guys would be lucky to date you."

"Right back at you, Flo."

I smile but know I haven't made the usual effort with my appearance. Whereas Sammy is dressed in a pretty summer dress paired with low slung sandals, her hair newly washed and face made up to perfection, I am dressed in shorts and a t-shirt with my hair scraped back in a ponytail and a face devoid of nothing but sunscreen.

We head nervously into the bar and are greeted by a smiling man and woman who hand us both a brightly coloured cocktail.

"Welcome, ladies." The man smiles warmly and says, "I'm Bobby and this is Imogen. Grab a seat, stand, whatever you fancy and try to relax. We will explain how this works when everyone's here."

We take our glasses and head into the bar and Sammy whispers, "My legs are shaking. I can't believe I'm so nervous. Thank God you came with me, I'd be a nervous wreck."

"To be honest, I'm questioning my own sanity right now."

We quickly grab a table in the corner of the bar, obscured by a rather large ficus tree, fake probably, and peer out as if we're two nervous explorers watching for something that might eat us alive.

"Do you see anyone you like the look of yet?"

Sammy whispers as if we're in the Serengeti and she doesn't want to alert the wildlife to our existence.

"No, have you?"

"No."

Sammy slumps in her seat and sighs. "There's still hope I suppose. I mean, most of the people here look ok I guess but nothing out of the ordinary."

"What were you expecting, Prince Charming?"

She nods. "Actually, yes I was."

We sip our cocktails and glance around with interest and soon catch the eye of a man who appears to be finding this as excruciating as we are. He looks normal enough, dressed in smart chinos and a polo shirt with his dark brown hair gelled slightly on top and if I had to guess I would say he's probably in his late thirties.

I catch his eye and he smiles, and before I can look away, heads purposefully towards us.

Sammy looks up with interest as he stops by the table and smiles. "Hi, I hope you don't mind but I'm feeling like a spare part out there. I don't suppose I could join you?"

Sammy nods and shifts along a little. "Of course, please take a seat."

He sits down and grins. "I am questioning my sanity right now."

"Same."

Sammy looks at him with interest. "I'm Sammy Jo and this is my friend Florrie."

"Ben."

He smiles, and it strikes me how nice he seems and I relax a little.

"Are you here on your own, Ben?"

"Yes, I decided to do this against my better judgement. Then I decided I needed to meet some new people and thought this would be a fun way to find some."

Sammy looks interested. "You're very brave coming on holiday on your own. I'm not sure I could do it."

"If I didn't, I wouldn't have a life." He looks at me and says with interest, "What about you, no husband, boyfriend or other?"

"No, sadly."

I smile as he grins. "It's not easy, is it – meeting someone that is? To be honest, I've tried everything. The internet, blind dates set up by friends, bars, clubs and even haunting the local supermarket in the hope someone will catch my eye in the veg aisle."

We laugh and I feel myself relaxing a little. Ben seems a normal enough guy, not weird at all, and makes me feel a little better about my decision.

"So, what do you do for a living?" Sammy says with interest, and he sighs. "I'm a dentist."

"Good job." She looks impressed, and I can see why. On the outside Ben looks like a real catch. Well dressed, smart, good personality and a job with prospects. Maybe there's something in this after all.

"What about you?" Ben smiles at her and she laughs. "Unemployed as of a few days ago. Florrie persuaded me to give up my job and come away with her and I didn't take much persuading."

Ben looks a little shocked. "That was, um, extremely brave of you."

She shrugs. "Not really, I hated my job and Florrie has promised to hire me if it comes down to it."

He turns his attention to me. "What do you do to earn a living?"

"I'm a beautician. I have my own mobile business, it's not ground breaking or anything but pays the bills."

Before he can answer, we hear a loud, "Welcome to cruising in love. I'm Bobby and this is my glamorous assistant, Imogen."

He looks around him happily and grins. "Today is all about relaxing and feeling comfortable. Check out the ship – each other..." he laughs and there is a low rumble of laughter in the room. "We have your preferences, and the computer is matching you up as we speak. However..."

He lowers his voice. "If you see anyone you absolutely must meet, have a word with myself or Imogen and we will play cupid and offer a helping hand along the way."

Imogen nods, and Bobby claps his hands. "This is so exciting. I can feel it in my bones, this is going to be a love cruise like no other."

Sammy shakes her head as Ben shivers a little. For some reason I feel a little detached from the whole situation because I'm here physically, but mentally I'm somewhere else entirely and I wonder if this was such a good idea. I have zero enthusiasm for this and don't think it's fair on whoever they pair me with.

I notice Sammy looking around with interest and note that Ben looks to be doing the same. I couldn't care less and feel more interested in grabbing another cocktail and wonder if I should be seriously worried right now about my sanity and desire for alcohol.

After a while, Ben says with a sigh, "Well, I suppose I should mingle a little before heading to my sun-bed. What are your plans for today?"

"Same." I look at Sammy, and she nods. "Yes, I am definitely going to work on my tan and see what else this fun palace has to offer."

Ben stands and smiles warmly. "Well, I wish you both every success in your quest to find the perfect man. If there is such a thing of course."

He walks away, and Sammy looks a little confused. "He didn't seem interested in us which has crushed my self-confidence already."

"Maybe we're not his type." I shrug, and she shakes her head. "Then I wonder what is because I haven't seen anyone who could hold a candle to us, in my opinion, anyway."

Watching Ben move through the room, I wonder what he's looking for. "It takes all sorts, Sammy, and maybe he has a firm image in his mind of what he wants and we're not measuring up to that. Perhaps it's not attraction he's after but someone on his level. A fellow professional maybe, someone to settle down with."

"You could be right. Maybe I should have embellished the truth a little and fabricated a wild and interesting story of the person I would rather be than the one I am."

"What, lie?" I shake my head. "That would only end in

tears. I mean, if you did and then really fell for a guy and had to come clean, it would start things off on the wrong footing. The trust would be destroyed before it even started, and how can you move on from that? No, be honest because the right man will want you regardless of what job you do, how much money you earn, or where you live. Don't waste time on those who wouldn't because they don't deserve you, anyway."

She nods, but I'm not sure if she agreed with what I said because my friend has that look in her eye that spells trouble ahead. This may not turn out well after all.

10

The wind whips around my sun-bed like a mother fussing over her young and I shiver a little.

"I thought it would be warmer than this."

Sammy groans. "I'm freezing which is a serious problem because I was hoping to get a selfie for Instagram in my neon orange bikini just to make everyone jealous that I'm living my best life."

Shivering, I pull my towel a little tighter around my shoulders and stare at the hordes of other sunbathers who are bracing the elements on the sundeck beside the Olympic-sized pool. Only the sound of screaming children drowns out the moans from some very disappointed passengers who expected the sunshine to have been booked for the duration of the voyage.

"I'm not sure I feel so great, Flo."

Sammy does look a little green, and as the ship lurches a little on the swell, I watch as she closes her eyes and leans back in her seat.

"Why can't I stop thinking of what I ate for breakfast?"

"Maybe you should take a sea sickness tablet; I have some in my bag."

"I'll take three."

Without opening her eyes, Sammy holds out her hand and I say bluntly, "You can have one, and then drag yourself up and look at the horizon. I heard that helps because it focuses your mind on something other than extreme movement."

The ship lurches again, and the breeze picks up and Sammy clutches her hand to her mouth before jumping up and hanging off the edge, meeting her breakfast for the second time today.

The woman next to us turns her back as Sammy's retching can be heard above the wind.

A man stops by and shakes his head. "I'm guessing this is her first time at sea. What she needs is a ginger biscuit."

"I'm not sure food is the answer in this situation." I stare at him in horror as he laughs.

"Trust me, I never set sail without a few packets of the ginger stuff. Here, I always have some close to hand during the first few days."

He rummages in his bag and offers me a handful of biscuits. "Here, have one yourself, it helps you know."

The woman turns around and nods. "He's right, love, sometimes the strangest things are what's needed."

"Oh, well, ok, thanks."

I take the biscuits and head over to Sammy, who is now crying. "I'm going to die. I must have eaten a poisonous egg at breakfast."

"Don't be so dramatic." I slip her a biscuit and say firmly, "Here, eat this and stare at the horizon. The tablet won't act immediately and you need to get a grip."

Once again, she hurls overboard and I just hope nobody catches any of it as they recline on their balcony below.

Sammy shivers as she retches some more and now I'm feeling decidedly ill myself as I shiver beside her as the ship rocks and the wind blows.

She thankfully shoves the biscuit in her mouth, giving me time to dive for my towel and wrap it around me like a cape. "I'm not cut out for this, Florrie, I never packed my sea legs."

"You'll be fine." I'm starting to feel decidedly sick myself by now but that all gets pushed aside when I hear a loud, "Sandy!"

I look up in the direction of the voice and see a man standing nearby, looking at my friend in disbelief. She turns around and I feel a little sympathetic when I see vomit sticking to her hair and biscuit crumbs mixed with saliva on her lips. Then she yells so loud it hurts my ears, "Danny!!"

Looking between them, I wonder if I've fallen into some warped version of Grease right now because surely Danny and Sandy were the stars of Summer Loving.

I watch as a fascinated observer as they stare at one another with a mixture of joy and euphoria wrapped up in a whole lot of tension.

It's interesting to watch the surprise dim and an awkward atmosphere to invade the crazy mixed up space as Sandy, aka Sammy Jo, says rather coolly, "It's been what, four years?"

Two months, five days and three hours, judging by the hurt in her eyes. I am a fascinated spectator as he looks at her rather sheepishly. "I can't believe it's you."

Looking back to my friend, I feel a surge of sympathy at how she looks right now. Her bikini is decorated with vomit and her skin resembles cobblestones as she shivers in the icy wind. Her mouth is encrusted in God only knows what, and her hair whips around her like Medusa's snakes. Her eyes look hurt and frantic as if she is struggling to make sense of what's happening right now and she whispers, "So, um, how are you?"

It strikes me that the cure for sea sickness appears to be in the form of a rather hot looking guy, who is looking at Sandy/Sammy as if he can't quite believe his eyes.

"I'm good thanks, are you?"

I almost want to laugh out loud because it's pretty obvious right now my friend is anything but fine, but she nods as if in a daze and attempts to smile. "Yes, um, good."

He laughs a little awkwardly. "So, this is weird. I mean, we haven't seen each other for years and now, here we are."

"Yes, we are here."

For some reason Sammy is voicing words that are lacking any thought behind them because she is staring at hot guy as if she doesn't know what to make of it. I feel the need to interrupt and say brightly, "Hi, I'm Florence, Sammy's friend, how do you two know one another?"

He shakes himself and offers a tense smile. "Sorry, I'm Joseph, we um, worked together when we were sixteen, for how many years?" He turns his attention to Sammy again, and I'm surprised to see a yearning in his eyes that he is struggling to get under control.

Sammy nods. "We worked together at Sainsburys while we were at college. That seems so long ago now."

He nods and can't appear to tear his eyes away from her and not just because she is turning blue from the cold and looks like an alien from the planet disaster.

Feeling the need to protect her from what is obviously an extremely excruciating reunion, I say briskly, "Anyway, as I'm sure you can tell, my friend isn't feeling so good right now and I should get her cleaned up and into something warm."

He almost shakes himself and then to my surprise, steps forward and wraps his towel around a shivering Sammy.

"Of course, I'm sorry. Please, let me help."

She nods, apparently still in shock and the concern in his eyes melts my heart a little.

"I could fetch you a coffee, brandy perhaps…"

"No." She looks slightly alarmed. "Thank you."

She steps back a little. "I really should be getting back to my cabin. It was nice to see you, Joe, or should I say, Danny."

A little of the old Sammy resurfaces for a second and I don't miss the long lingering look they share as a pleasant memory revisits them.

He makes to speak, but she cuts him off sharply. "So, we should go, thanks for the towel, Joe." She shrugs out of it and he shakes his head. "Keep it, I'll get another, no problem."

I don't blame him because anything could be on that towel now, and Sammy nods. "Great. Um, well, we should, um, go."

Stepping in to end this weird, awkward conversation, I gently guide her away from a man who is struggling with his emotions right now and as we walk away, I say firmly, "This is one story I can't wait to hear."

11

Sammy Jo is quiet, and not just because of her sickness. We made it back to the cabin without incident, and I waited on the balcony while she showered and changed. Setting out the rest of the medicinal ginger biscuits, I grab a bottle of water from the minibar and settle down to wait for her to spill the beans because there is most definitely a story waiting to be told.

As I wait, it strikes me how freeing this whole experience is. I am sitting on a ship's balcony with nothing but water as far as the eye can see. Just thinking of Oliver tucked up back in England with his new wife makes this even more surreal somehow.

Part of me is so angry with him. I feel used, betrayed and cast aside, but alongside those feelings I feel relief more than anything. Relief that I am free of a situation that was becoming a very bad idea. Picturing Oliver beside me on this honeymoon cruise is strange because it's as if he's a stranger to me now. Imagining him opposite me, probably moaning about the weather and attacking the mini bar before morning coffee is not a pleasant image. He would spend most of the trip in the casino. I have no doubt about that and I'm guessing we would have a few arguments before the fortnight is out.

Married life after ten years would be ours after ten minutes. Is that what happens when you commit to the wrong mistake? A lifetime of tense conversations and the cold shoulder rather than admit you made a mistake in the first place. I am guilty of that more than anyone because I know I was only going through with the whole charade, so I didn't let my family down. However, I let myself down and part of me admires Oliver for acting on impulse and setting us both free.

Does love make a person irrational? Is it a life changing moment when you meet 'the one' because I certainly hope so? Is my 'one' on this ship, or have I yet to meet him? Looking at Sammy and Joseph something tells me there's a lot of unfinished business there and I wonder what happened in the past to make them look so – traumatised, really.

"That's better."

The woman herself heads onto the balcony, rubbing her wet hair with a towel and looking more like her normal self.

"Thanks, Florrie, I wouldn't have made it without you."

"It was nothing."

Sliding the plate of biscuits towards her, she grabs one and looks thoughtful.

"I can't believe I saw Joseph today. I never saw that one coming?"

"Who is he?" I lean slightly forward because it's obvious he's somebody important from her past.

She sighs heavily and looks out to sea, and for the first time since I've known her, she looks as if she's struggling.

"Joseph was my first unrequited love."

"Sounds complicated."

"It is." She slumps back in her seat and stares at the horizon. Although I'm doubting it's for medicinal reasons this time because it's as if she's searching for solutions as far as the crow flies.

"We worked together every Saturday in the superstore near my home. It was just us, locked away in the warehouse, filling trollies and generally fooling around, and I never saw him as anything other than a colleague. Maybe because we worked so closely, who knows but for some reason I couldn't see how amazing he really was."

"How long ago was that?"

"Five years ago, I think. Week in, week out, we worked side by side and only a chance remark from a friend of mine made me look at him a little differently."

She sighs and takes a small bite of her biscuit and looks troubled and I say with curiosity, "What's all the Danny and Sandy nonsense?"

She grins and I watch as a pleasant memory revisits her.

"We talked a lot of nonsense when we were working and discovered a shared love of Grease. We used to sing the songs and mimic the characters and one of our favourites was when they met again at the game. It was stupid really, but we called each other Danny and Sandy from that day forward. It didn't mean anything, as I said, it was stupid really."

"It sounds ok, just a bit of fun."

"Yeah, it was fun. To be honest, I started looking forward to going to work. I loved spending time with him and our friendship grew into something more – at least *I* thought so."

"What happened?"

"It was my final day at Sainsburys. I was moving on to

the heady heights of a full-time job at the factory. College was over and I had bills to pay. I couldn't afford to further my education and I had to pay my way at home because my dad lost his job and money was tight."

"I'm sorry, it must have been tough."

She sighs and smiles brightly. "It was fine. I was never academic anyway. So, we were heading to a party later. One of the other girls was having it and my leaving was just a coincidence. Well, we were all going, and I was looking forward to it because Joseph was going to be there and I hadn't seen him outside of work before. Unfortunately, when we arrived, he had his tongue down the girl's throat who was holding the party."

"I'm sorry, Sammy."

"It was fine. It made me face up to a few things, you know, knock the cobwebs off my fairy story and remind me I'm no princess."

"You are – an amazing princess, to me anyway."

She laughs softly. "Spoken like a true friend. Well, I tried to have a good time, but it was difficult watching him lurch from one available girl to the next. You know, red flags surrounded him because he was on a mission to snog every girl in the room, it seems. Well, by the time I was leaving he looked sicker than I was back there and as I went to pass, he grabbed hold of me and pushed me up against the wall. I know it was irresponsible of me but this was my last chance and I'm ashamed to admit I kissed the life out of that boy. In fact, it was the hottest kiss I have ever experienced and I regret nothing."

She shrugs but if her expression is anything to go by, she regrets everything and I nod to show some moral support.

"You have nothing to be ashamed about. If anyone does, it's him."

"Maybe, but you see it never went anywhere past that moment because my cab arrived and my friends called me to heel. My last sighting of Joseph was sitting outside on the wall with his head in his hands as we drove away and that was the last I saw of him until today."

We fall silent because if I'm honest, it's not exactly what I thought I'd hear and almost as if she can read minds she laughs bitterly, "It's hardly a love story, is it? Now the tables have turned, and he's seen *me* at my worst. Just my luck. After all these years, the one who got away returned at the worst possible moment and he is probably lowering the life boat as we speak in a bid to create as much distance between us as possible."

A loud knock interrupts our conversation and I quickly run to answer it, leaving Sammy to slump miserably in her seat.

I notice a slip of paper posted underneath the door and, grabbing it quickly, scan the words.

Your dream date awaits Sammy Jo. Meet Pierre in the Condor lounge at 3pm for an informal chat.

There is a second piece of paper stapled to it and my heart rate increases as a similar message bears my name.

Your dream date awaits Florence. Meet Norman in the Crystal rooms at 3pm for an informal chat.

Suddenly, I feel sicker than Sammy Jo was just one hour ago. Norman doesn't sound promising at all. At least Pierre may be a super-sexy French man and visions of Sammy Jo's date shape up way better than the one I have of my impending nightmare. I'm not sure why a name defines a person, but I can't push the disappointment down that my first date is probably with a man old enough to be my father.

Sammy looks up when I head onto the balcony trying to look as if I'm happy about this and she squeals when she sees her invite and looks up, her eyes shining.

"Pierre. Oh, my goodness, he is bound to be super-sexy and French. Just the accent alone will be worth this whole experience. Do you think he's tall, dark and handsome, I ordered one of those you know?"

"Didn't we all."

I hand her my sheet and she fights to stop the giggles from revealing she is of much of the same mind as I am.

"Norman, well, he sounds interesting."

"In what way?" I feel a headache coming on as she says thoughtfully, "Probably a lord, a duke perhaps. He has a sprawling country estate in the highlands and a chic pad in Chelsea. Undoubtedly in banking, probably gentry and is taking a trip to find the next Lady or Duchess to help him spend his millions."

"In a check shirt with a rifle slung over his shoulder, probably dining on pheasant and stoking the fire of a crumbling ruin that is cold and dark in the winter and musty in the summer. Then again, he could be a nervous type who lives with his mother and collects butterflies in his spare time. I think I'd prefer Pierre to be honest."

She starts to giggle and despite my horror at the situation I find myself in, I have to laugh. Let the game commence.

12

I make my way to the Crystal rooms, having left a very excited Sammy Jo heading in the opposite direction. I'm not feeling it though and wish more than anything I was shivering on my deckchair in a storm, rather than facing an hour of dull conversation with a man I know in my heart already is not for me. In fact, it's got nothing to do with his name, it's me. I'm not ready to meet anyone, it's too soon and I feel like a fraud. A desperate fraud because how is this a good thing for either of us? The poor man must be looking for the woman of his dreams, and I'm not up for that.

The Crystal rooms is an amazing bar area designed to sparkle in every way it can. Chandeliers twinkle above a polished marble floor. Mirrors decorated in fake diamonds hug the walls and reflect my misery as I look at a woman who is way out of her comfort zone right now. It has a beautiful mirrored bar that runs the length of a small wall to the side and clear glass tables are set around a place that wouldn't look out of place in Cinderella's palace.

I notice Bobby waiting anxiously by the door, clipboard in hand, and he smiles as I approach.

"Florence, darling, you look like an angel. Welcome."

I resist rolling my eyes because if he considers this an amazing outfit, he's delusional. I didn't even try and just pulled on a pair of denim shorts with a red t-shirt with the wording, 'Keep Calm and Drink Champagne' decorating the front and I smile nervously as he points to a table in the corner of the room.

"Your date is waiting." he looks down at his clipboard. "Oh yes, Norman Fielding, a nice chap, you should get on."

Should, or hope, I'm not sure if he's saying that to make himself feel better because even from here, I can see my fears were well-founded. Norman doesn't look as if he can be my dad, he could be my grandad.

Bobby sighs and looks a little apologetic and whispers, "It will be fine, you wait, Norman's a real character, you should have fun."

Sighing, I just nod and taking a deep breath, I head across to spend one hour in dullsville.

He looks up as I approach and I hate the way he looks at me, his eyes firmly glued to the wording on my chest before running down the rest of my body. Wishing I'd worn a maxi dress at least, I quickly slide into the seat opposite and smile.

"Hi, Norman, isn't it?"

"It sure is and you must be Florence. Well, I must say I'm pleasantly surprised."

"Um, thank you."

He hands me a glass of champagne and winks. "At least I know this is your tipple, your preference is written across your chest."

Once again, his eyes drift lazily across my breasts and I feel a shiver pass through me as I contemplate drowning him in the champagne in the not-so-distant future.

"So, um, Norman, this is nice. What brought you to the Aphrodite?"

He smiles, revealing a yellowing set of teeth that looks as if he has a dental aversion and says, "I like to cruise, it's one of the few holidays a single man can go on and meet several interesting people. You know, it's a good place to make new friends and form attachments. So, what about you, my dear, what brings you looking for love?"

"I'm not."

He raises his eyes and I think fast. "Actually, love is the furthest thing from my mind."

"Then why did you sign up for cruising in love?"

He looks confused and I think fast. "Research."

"For what?"

"For my, um, blog. Yes, that's it, I'm an influencer, a travel and beauty one and I'm here to blow the lid on everything cruising."

He looks disappointed and I feel bad about that as he leans back and starts scanning the room for other potential love interests.

"Interesting. I'm not sure the organisers would be impressed though."

"Why not?"

"Because it's a little dishonest, really. You see, here I was waiting to meet the woman of my dreams and she walked in. I must tell you I was more than interested, my darling, and you just have to say the word and I'll be ordering another key card to my room with your name on it."

"Excuse me."

I look at him in horror, and he leans forward and grins, making me feel slightly nauseous. "I won't tell if you won't. What do you say, join me for a little excitement and we'll keep it our little secret? It could be fun."

He winks, and I set my glass down on the table and say tightly. "It's an emphatic no. To be honest, if that's all you're here for, I'm leaving."

He laughs as if I've said something hilarious. "Darling, it's all anyone is here for. Open your eyes and sharpen your pencil because it's obvious you were born yesterday. These cruising programs are nothing more than an excuse for single people to enjoy two weeks of sun, sea, adventure and sex. Lots of it in fact. It's what keeps us coming back for more every year. If you really thought you would meet Prince Charming on board, then you're delusional. Write that in your blog, the realities of cruising today. Trust me, I'm a regular."

He grips his champagne and tosses it back and then leans forward, whispering, "So, what do you say, an afternoon of fun in my cabin with no recriminations? You *will* have fun; I promise you that at least and nobody need know."

"Excuse me, I think I'm going to be sick."

I scrape back my chair and without even looking at the creep, I head off purposefully, my anger growing with every stride. How dare he. Just the thought of it is making me feel like jumping overboard. I knew this was a bad idea and part of me feels like hunting my friend down before she decides to take some French lothario up on a similar offer. So much for cruising in love, more like cruising into a nightmare.

Bobby looks worried as I pass and I say tightly, "I'm sorry, Bobby. That man is disgusting. He doesn't want to find love; he just wants to find someone to have sex with. Don't bother sending me on any more dates if that's what this is all about."

Bobby, to his credit, looks absolutely horrified and pulls me to one side.

"What do you mean, what happened?"

I quickly fill him in and he looks so upset some of my anger diminishes a little.

"Leave it with me, Florence. I'll pull him from the programme. Thank you for letting me know."

As I walk away, I wonder if I overreacted a little. Maybe this is what happens at sea. It worked for Oliver, it seems. A quick gamble with love and hey presto, soulmate. Is this really what love is these days? Sample the goods before finding out who is offering them? If I felt disillusioned before, nothing prepared me for how I'm feeling now and as I walk blindly through the large palatial rooms to God only knows where, I wish I was anywhere else but here.

13

Sammy, it appears, had the opposite experience to mine and arrives back in our room in a haze of lust and excitement.

"Wow, Florrie, Pierre was amazing, you should have been there."

"Really, in what way?"

Just from the sparkle in her eyes I can tell he sprinkled a little bit of lust dust in them and she sits on the bed and hugs herself. "Well, the French accent is sexy enough, but the man it belonged to was intense. I mean, really intense."

"In what way?" I am so excited to hear this story because I'm hoping it restores my faith in men that is slipping away from me with every minute that ticks by.

"He was in his thirties, I think, and owns a company exporting wine. He speaks really good English with an accent that makes me forget my own name. You know, I think I hit the jackpot on the first throw."

"I'm pleased for you. What happens now?"

If anything, I hope he is her 'one' because then we could pull out of this quite frankly ridiculous programme.

"Well, I make a note that I'm interested in him and if he does the same, we are classed as a perfect match. There are still six more contenders and let me tell you, if they are as gorgeous as he is I'm going to have a very difficult decision to make."

She looks at me with interest. "How was your date?"

I fill her in, and she stares at me in horrified outrage. "You're kidding?"

"No, I'm not, and quite frankly I'm considering withdrawing, anyway. I knew it was a bad idea."

"Don't you dare. One bad apple doesn't always infect the barrel. Somewhere inside is the man you were meant to find; trust me I know about these things."

"And Joseph, what if he's one of my dates, would you be so encouraging then?"

It's as if I've pierced a blade through her heart, because Sammy looks at me with a look of pure devastation.

"Do you think he signed up, what if we're matched?"

"It's a possibility."

I'm surprised the thought never occurred to her because it was the first thing that struck me.

"But, surely he's with someone. He may not be here on his own. Not Joseph, he's probably married by now, anyway."

"What makes you so sure, maybe he thinks the same?"

Sammy shakes her head and I regret bringing the subject up at all because the spark in her eyes has dimmed and she looks nervous. "I'm not sure I can deal with how I feel about him. I know it's stupid really, but he makes me question every decision I've ever made. I threw myself at him at that party, Florrie. Do you know how mortified I was when the cold light of day reminded me? Thank goodness I never had to face him again, and then fate made sure I faced my mistake at my lowest point. It's Karma you know. I did something foolish, and it's come back to bite me. How can I ever face him again after what we did?"

"You did nothing, Sammy. For goodness' sake, it was a drunken kiss at a party, it's hardly grounds for life imprisonment for sullying your reputation. I fail to see what the problem is, in fact, it may be nice to catch up and rekindle an old flame."

"It's not just that though."

A cold feeling washes over me as I see something in my friend's eyes that she is struggling to keep hidden.

"What is it?"

I hold my breath as she places her head in her hands and says, "I made a fool of myself."

"In what way?"

She groans and leans back on the bed and places a pillow over her head. "I called him the next day and asked him out. I told him to pick me up at seven and we could go and talk about our future."

"And did he?"

"No. he never showed up. So I phoned him again and shouted down the phone that I never wanted to see him again and men like him weren't worth the bother."

"So why is that bad?"

"Because the girl whose party it was phoned me a few hours later. She gloated down the phone and told me to stop embarrassing myself and leave her boyfriend alone. They had come home and found my desperate attempt to make him mine and had a good laugh about it. Apparently, he was embarrassed that I even thought I stood a chance with him and he asked her to warn me off."

"That's terrible." I stare at her in horror, and she groans. "It's taken me five years to get over the humiliation and embarrassment and all I can think of is what if she's here too? What if they got married and started a family? How will I feel when I see them all happy and together when my life is a mess? I need this cruising in love programme, Florence, because I need to prove to them that I'm over him and under someone else."

Images of Norman swim into view and I feel my soul shiver when I think of Sammy anywhere near that man.

Instead, I sigh and say brightly, "Then we need to find you a man and fast. If that's the kind of guy Joseph is then you had a lucky escape anyway and if we do see that girl from the party, you will make it your business to prove that you are better than her in every way possible."

"I'm hoping we don't – see them that is."

"We probably won't because this ship is huge and I haven't even seen Ellen and Geoffrey and who could miss them? No, we'll be fine. Two women on a quest for happiness and that doesn't need to include a man. We have an adventure waiting for us and nothing is going to get in the way of that, trust me.

14

We finally catch up with Ellen and Geoffrey when we head to the theatre to watch Mamma Mia after dinner. On our way in, I hear a familiar, "Honestly, Geoffrey, you should never have eaten that third helping. At this rate, I will need to order the buggy to come and wheel you to the stateroom. First thing tomorrow you are signing up for body blast, no arguments."

"Hi, Ellen, Geoffrey."

I turn and smile at the couple who are looking amazing, dressed to impress in their finest cocktail wear.

"Darling, how lovely to see you."

She air kisses both of us and smiles. "I was only saying to Geoffrey over dinner that we hadn't seen you since muster. How are things, have you found the men of your dreams yet?"

"I have, two actually and counting." Sammy grins and I can tell Ellen's impressed. "Super darling, I feel like a proud mother. Word of advice, don't just stop at two. The voyage is still in its infancy and there may be more rich pickings ahead."

She turns her attention to me and says rather sharply, "So, you're falling behind. Is there a problem we need to address?"

"Only if you can create a force field around me, keeping creepy men old enough to my grandfather away. Quite honestly, Ellen, I may never recover from what I've experienced so far."

She looks horrified and yet a little interested at the same time, and I feel quite disturbed as she pulls me to one side. "So, this man, tell me about him."

"Well, he was only interested in one thing, no questions asked activity in his stateroom. Honestly, Ellen, it was most disturbing."

"Interesting. Maybe you should point him out to me when you see him. I'll get Geoffrey to have a word."

"It's fine, I told cruise ship Bobby, and he promised he would take him off the programme."

"Yes, quite right." She looks around. "I don't suppose he's here in the crowd perhaps. Have a good look my dear, he could be watching us as we speak."

Glancing around, I sincerely hope he's not because I never want to see that man again - ever.

However, I do see someone that makes my heart beat a little faster and my breath hitch because sitting on the edge of a row looking at his phone is the man I met as we set sail, Marcus.

Ellen must see my expression change because she looks across and whispers, "Do you know that man?"

"Not really."

"Ah, an encounter. I've had many of those."

She looks impressed. "A fine specimen, my dear. If I was five years younger, I would fight you for him."

She winks as I look at her in astonishment, and despite my shock, I giggle at the wicked glint in her eye.

"Maybe you should brush past him, there are a few seats in his row, she who dares wins after all."

She does have a point and I feel a little twinge of excitement as I whisper back, "That's not such a bad idea. Would you care to join us?"

"We are right in front of you darling."

I must look confused because she whispers, "We'll go first, that way you can be last, and grab the seat next to him. You've got to be calculating about affairs of the heart you know."

She turns to Geoffrey and says loudly, "I feel like a change tonight, I think we should view the show from..." she looks around and then says triumphantly, "That row over there. Lead on Geoffrey and make haste, the show is about to start."

She winks as she passes, and Sammy looks worried. "Oh no, is it? I was going to grab some popcorn; do you think I have time?"

"Yes, of course. shall I follow them and grab those seats while you get the snacks?"

"Good idea, Florrie, you know, I am loving everything about this cruise so far. Just make sure you keep those sea sickness tablets coming. We definitely do not need a repeat performance of the disaster from earlier."

She heads off and for some reason, I feel a little vulnerable right now. Maybe I should forget about men until my heart and pride have healed because the last thing I need is another setback but this man is playing heavily on my mind and I need to get him out of my system urgently.

I follow Ellen and hear Geoffrey say loudly, "Excuse me, are these seats taken?"

I daren't even look as Marcus jumps up and says politely, "No, be my guest."

Geoffrey and Ellen walk past and I'm not sure if it was on purpose or not, but Ellen stumbles a little and ends up clinging to Marcus for support.

"Oh, I'm so sorry my dear, my sea legs aren't what they used to be."

"Don't worry, here, let me help you."

I watch in disbelief as he helps her to her seat and before he leaves, she says loudly, "Sorry, I have two friends joining us. Florence darling, over here."

I am so glad it's dark in here because I feel very heated when he looks my way and I see the recognition in his eyes.

A lazy smile breaks across his face and his eyes gleam as he offers me his hand.

"Allow me to steady you."

As I reach out, I love the way his large hand closes around mine, and he pulls me gently to meet him. I can feel Ellen watching me like a hawk as I say quickly, "Um, thank you, you are very kind."

I have to push past him in the row to reach my seat and he says in a low voice, "We meet again."

"Yes, um, we do, so, how is your cruise?"

"Enjoyable so far. How about you?"

"Yes, um, same."

I feel myself blushing furiously and hate this person I've become. Obviously, I've been fantasising about him when I have no reason to, because I shouldn't be affected by any man right now.

He gestures to the seat beside him and says huskily, "It would be good if you could join me and maybe your friend can take the one beside you."

I nod shyly and catch Ellen smirking and giving me the

thumbs up as she nudges Geoffrey and whispers something in his ear. He looks across and nods and then turns his attention back to the stage.

Marcus regards me with an intensity I'm unaccustomed to and whispers, "I was hoping to run into you."

"Really." My mouth is dry, and I am struggling to form a coherent sentence around him.

"Yes, I may be able to push some business your way, if you're interested that is."

"Like what?"

This is surprising, and he nods, looking pleased with himself. "When you mentioned your friend was out of a job, it got me thinking. I always have an opening for presentable women, or men, to act as guides in my online presentations. Do you think it's something that would interest you?"

"Possibly."

We look up as Sammy arrives, hiding behind huge cartons of popcorn and soft drinks and we stand so she can squeeze into the seat beside me.

"Goodness, I thought I'd miss the show, the queue was so long and the guy in front of me was taking so long."

Luckily the music starts, which gives me a bit of breathing space because suddenly my faith has been restored – work for Marcus, now that's an interesting proposition I'm happy about.

15

I was absolutely blown away by the show and we could have been sitting in the West End because the show we just witnessed would rival any they perform there.

Sammy appears to have got over her seasickness and has polished off a large bucket of popcorn and is now ripping open a packet of peanuts. I feel a little uncomfortable now that the lights have come on, because I'm not sure I can ever look Marcus in the eye again.

The fact we know every Abba song ever written didn't make for easy listening for the people who surrounded us and the fact we were so loud about it drew many concerned looks our way. I think I caught a man a few rows away filming us and expect we will be viral on Tiktok by the time we leave the auditorium.

"You're wasted."

Marcus laughs like a low rumble of thunder, and I shake my head. "Not really, I only had one glass of wine with my meal, I'm pacing myself."

He laughs softly. "Not drunk. I mean, you're wasted as a

beautician. You should be starring in these shows, not watching then."

I stare at him in surprise, looking for a hint of sarcasm in his expression, but he genuinely seems impressed which makes me feel quite good about myself.

"Do you think?"

"Of course."

We share a rather intimate look and I feel a shiver pass through me as I drown in his lustful eyes and he whispers, "Would you like to meet me for a drink one evening, maybe tomorrow night? Do you think your friend would mind?"

Hearing Sammy laugh at something Ellen is saying, I feel a little guilty. Then again, Sammy is probably lining up drinks dates as we speak and so I nod a little shyly. "I'd like that."

"Then shall we say 8 o'clock in the piano bar?"

"Sounds lovely."

He smiles and I have to pinch myself that this is happening at all. Marcus is the type of guy I imagine hangs out with models or actresses. Not women like me who look more at home in jogging bottoms and printed t-shirts, watching Netflix with a box of Maltesers.

He stands and smiles. "Have a good evening, I'll look forward to seeing you again tomorrow."

He heads off and Ellen sighs. "That man is a dream."

Geoffrey looks a little put out. "Steady on, Ellen, I am here you know."

"Don't remind me." Ellen rolls her eyes and Sammy nudges me sharply, stifling a giggle which almost sets me off too.

We all vacate our seats and head outside and Ellen asks with interest, "So, was project gorgeous guy a success?"

"Well, if you must know I'm having drinks with him tomorrow night in the piano bar."

Sammy looks like a proud mother and hugs me hard. "Way to go Florrie, I knew you would see the light. I feel a bit annoyed that I never got a good look at him now."

"You don't mind then."

"Of course I don't mind. Why would I?"

"Because I'll be leaving you alone."

"Hardly. I bumped into Tony when I went for popcorn. He told me he has tomorrow night off and would I like to discuss cruising options over dinner."

"Sammy!"

I stare at her in shock, and she shrugs. "He is quite gorgeous, and I did promise."

"But isn't there a rule about dating passengers somewhere in the crew bible?"

Ellen interrupts. "If there is, they are always breaking them. You know, I've had countless sailors, crew members and even the captain once, they're all at it and know many nooks and crannies where an illicit affair can be conducted in the utmost secrecy. I feel quite jealous really, it's what makes for a memorable trip."

Sammy looks impressed and I shake my head as Geoffrey says thoughtfully, "You know, I think they are warned off the guests but I had a massage once that turned into a very happy ending. Do you remember, Ellen, I told you about Heidi the Swiss Masseuse on the Princess of the Sea? Most enjoyable it was, and I was happy to contribute to her pension fund."

Ellen nods her approval and then says briskly, "Well, we should be going. I fancy a game of Roulette, darling, I'm feeling lucky tonight."

She smiles as she takes Geoffrey's hand. "Keep us posted,

darlings, and remember Florence, if you catch sight of that predatory man, snap a photo and ping it to me. Here's my number."

She hands me a gold embossed card with her contact details on and as she heads off, Sammy giggles. "Ellen is a wild card, Flo, I want to be just like her when I grow up."

"You have grown up, silly."

"Physically maybe, but mentally I'm struggling to make it out of puberty."

She grabs my hand and grins. "Come on, let's go and check out the eighties disco, I could party all night."

As she drags me off to dance the night away, my heart feels a little lighter somehow. This has been a good evening but tomorrow promises to be a day I may never forget.

16

The sun beats through the blinds and I groan as Sammy shouts, "Wake up, Florrie, we've arrived."

"Where?"

"Land. Nassau to be precise."

I open one sleepy eye and watch Sammy dragging several outfits out of the wardrobe and throwing them on the bed. "Which one do you think would look best on my Instagram feed."

She holds up a navy and white striped dress and a red scarf. "What about this?"

"A bit stereotypical nautical life if you ask me."

"Yes, I did wonder."

"Anyway..." I sit up and groan, running my fingers through my hair as if it will somehow wake my brain that appears to be still sleeping. "What time is it?"

"7 am."

"Are you serious?"

"Yes, we need to have breakfast and then disembark because I am not missing a minute of the Bahamas."

"But we only reached this bed at 3am. How will I operate today?"

"You'll manage. The adrenalin will kick in and there'll be no stopping you. Come on, Florrie, I'm starving and need to get going."

Groaning, I drag myself from my warm and cosy bed and into the shower, where I take a long leisurely wash in a frantic bid to wake myself up. Despite the early hour, I am also keen to experience the delights of the Bahamas and decide on a simple pale blue sundress with white espadrilles.

We head off to breakfast and note the air of excited chatter that is present today because this is the first stop on our magical tour and unlike yesterday, the sun has definitely got his hat on and is coming out to play.

By the time we grab our SeaPass and bags filled with towels, sunscreen and credit cards, we are both extremely excited as we head off in search of the exit.

The sun hits us as soon as we step foot on the gangplank and as we head onto shore, Sammy laughs happily. "This is the life, Florrie. You know I've always wanted to come here ever since I watched Pirates of the Caribbean. Do you think we'll find Jack Sparrow languishing in a bar somewhere? I certainly hope so."

"No, I'm guessing all we'll find is endless ways to spend our money and end up with tan lines where we don't need them."

"So, what shall we do, it's certainly hot already. Maybe find a spot on the beach?"

"Sounds good to me."

We head off in search of tropical paradise along with several hundred more passengers who are increasingly becoming a problem to me.

"You know, Sammy, I wish we could just find a little corner away from people. There are just so many of them all the time."

"Yes, it is a little overwhelming. Maybe we should just find a sheltered spot and relax for the day."

We start walking and despite my grumpy mood, I feel happy that we left the ship earlier than most. It does seem quieter without several thousand other people walking along beside us and as we start exploring a little piece of paradise, I feel myself relax for the first time in what feels like forever.

"You know, Florrie, I heard Johnny Depp bought a private island nearby. He fell in love with it while shooting Pirates of the Caribbean. Can you even imagine having your own island?"

"Can you imagine having Johnny Depp?"

"Only in my dreams darling." Sammy grins, and as we walk along the bright streets of Nassau, I can't think of a better companion to be with on this trip of a lifetime.

We see a sign for a water park that looks interesting and stop to take a look.

"Atlantic Aquaventure. Wow, Florrie, shall we go there, it looks like such fun and we could sunbathe too. I'm also guessing they have food; it could be just what we need."

"Ok, it sounds great."

"Spying a taxi nearby, we head towards it and before we know it, are whisked away to the nearest water park with a day of fun and excitement stretching before us.

By the time we return to the ship in the late afternoon we are both tired but buzzing with the amazing day we've had.

Soaking up the sun at the water park was just perfect, and an afternoon spent shopping in the amazing craft market was an experience I am unlikely to ever forget.

As we dress for dinner, I select my outfit carefully because of my 'date' with Marcus shortly afterwards. Deciding on a short black dress and matching wedges, I spray my favourite perfume and look at my reflection critically in the mirror.

"You look beautiful, Flo."

Catching sight of my friend, I smile. "You don't look so bad yourself."

Sammy looks like an angel. Her hair is brushed and touches her shoulders as if it has a life of its own. Her make up is subtle yet elegant and the white shift dress she is wearing is the perfect backdrop to the vibrant scarf she picked up in the market earlier. As days go this has been a good one and I am so grateful to be sharing it with my best friend.

"So, we both have a date tonight. Do you think we should have a code knock just in case?" She looks thoughtful, and I shrug. "What are you talking about?"

"Well, what if we get lucky? I would hate to interrupt you and vice versa."

"Sammy no! Absolutely not and don't you dare."

"What?" She looks at me innocently, and I fix her with my most disapproving look. "You will not be bringing any men to this cabin, and neither will I. Why would you even want to?"

"Because it's been so long and maybe I'm desperate."

She almost looks tortured, and I shake my head. "No. If you are looking for a husband, that's not the way to find him. What's wrong with intoxicating conversation and discovering what he's like as a person? Surely you need to find out if you actually like the guy first rather than rushing into things. No, Sammy, this is not a good idea and you must promise not to even think about entertaining a man in this cabin."

"Stateroom."

"Well, whatever it is. Promise me."

She sighs heavily and picks up her clutch bag. "Ok, but after seeing your date for the evening you keep telling yourself that because if I'm abstaining from the sins of the flesh, so are you."

"Fine. I was never going there in the first place."

"Fine, shall we go?"

Sammy raises her eyes, and I nod. "Ok, let's go and eat, although I'm not sure if I have an appetite now."

"Why, do you feel ill?"

"Sick with nerves actually."

I lean against the mirror and sigh. "What am I doing, Sammy? This isn't me. I shouldn't be dating a guy I've just met when the old one hasn't even updated his Facebook status."

"He has."

"What?" I stare at her in confusion.

"Updated his status. I was trawling through Facebook earlier and hit on his page. Oliver is now classed as married and there are pictures all over his timeline of him and Grace."

"Who?"

"His wife, silly. The rather rough looking substitute for you. I must say his taste has changed and I'm guessing his family isn't impressed."

"Show me."

Like a maniac, I lunge for her phone and she sighs before scrolling to the page and handing it to me.

I stare in horror at my ex-groom as he smiles at the camera with his head resting against a woman who looks even rougher than I remember. She has wild curly hair and scarlet red lipstick that makes her look a lot older than him. She has those giant gypsy hoop earrings and is wearing a dress that is obviously two sizes too small. It's quite a shock to see a woman who looks nothing like me on the arm of the man who graces most of my Facebook and Instagram feed and I feel sick when I see the obvious happiness in Oliver's eyes.

I sit down heavily on the bed, and it hits me hard. Oliver's in love. In love with somebody who looks nothing like me and despite everything, it's a hard thing to face.

"Are you ok, Florrie?"

Sammy sounds concerned as she wraps her arm around my shoulders, and just knowing she is here is enough to give me a little strength.

"It's a shock." My voice sounds nothing like me, and she nods. "I know. It was to me, and I wasn't marrying him. Do you think she drugged him? I can think of no other reason why he replaced you with her. Maybe she's into black magic and cast a spell on him. She does look a little like a witch and she may be a modern day one."

"He loves her, that's reason enough. I can see it in his eyes. He looks happier somehow. If you look at my photos, he doesn't look like this. Why didn't I see it before?"

"See what?"

She sounds confused and I say huskily, "That we were so wrong for each other."

"Maybe you did, but ignored that little doubtful voice in your head. Maybe you were swept away by events and thought you were happy and maybe it takes you by surprise when you meet someone more suited to you to show you the error of your ways. Oliver must have really wanted this woman – Grace. Perhaps it hit him hard and he would do anything to keep her. If anything, the way you gave him up so easily tells you it was the right thing to do – for both of you. I'm guessing it's only when you meet a man you connect with, like Oliver did Grace, you will really understand the power of love."

"Do you think I ever will?"

I feel so broken, so destroyed and want to do nothing more than take to my bed with a huge box of chocolates and a chick flick.

Sammy says rather sternly, "Pull yourself together and face life head on. Oliver has already, so Ellen's right, you have no time to waste. I'm not talking about meeting a man; you will when you're good and ready. I mean embrace this experience. Leave your troubles back in England and reinvent yourself. I know I have and let me tell you, it works – big time."

"What do you mean, what have you done?"

"Oh nothing, just a little expanding of the truth on my cruising in love application. Anyway, I have a date pre-Tony that I can't miss and we need to eat. So, pick yourself up and prepare to face the glorious banquet that's waiting for us."

"I hope you're just talking about the food."

"Food never even crossed my mind." She winks and despite my trauma, I laugh a little.

"That's better. Now, come on, if I'm not mistaken you also have a little pre-date to endure before the main course."

As I grab my bag, I try to push down my pain. Sammy's right, I do have a date courtesy of the cruising in love programme. Cocktails with Richard in the Starlight room. I certainly hope he's better than the last one.

17

The man waiting for me looks one hundred times better than the last one and stands gallantly as I make my way to the table, as directed by Imogen this time.

She was positively beaming when she whispered that she had a good feeling about this one and so I have some hope at least that this will be a better experience.

"You must be Florence, I'm Richard, I'm pleased to meet you."

He shakes my hand warmly and first impressions are good. He's tall, athletic looking, and dressed smartly in a blazer with beige chinos and a bright blue shirt. He looks to be in his mid-thirties, which isn't a deal breaker, and I feel myself relaxing as I slip into the seat opposite, clutching a margarita.

"So, Florence, this is all a little strange, isn't it? Do you come here often?"

He laughs and I smile, shaking my head. "No, it's my first time."

"A cruise virgin, how lovely."

"I suppose I am." He smiles and raises his glass to mine.

"Then to making this one you will never forget."

As we clink glasses, I relax a little. Yes, Richard is more my type and seems normal.

The conversation flows easily and I discover Richard is an accountant and lives in Weybridge, in Surrey. We discuss our jobs, likes and dislikes and then I say innocently, "So, I suppose this is the million-dollar question, are you single, married or dating?"

I watch in horror as his face falls and tears start to drip down his face like a leaking tap.

"I'm sorry, have I said something to upset you."

Grabbing the serviette, he dabs at his eyes and sniffs. "I thought I could do this, be strong and move on."

"From what?" I feel so sorry for Richard because he is crumbling before my eyes and he sniffs, "I'm sorry, Florence, this is what I'd hope to avoid. You see..." He sniffs again, and I watch as he empties his glass and raises his hand to signal the waiter for another.

"You see, I was very happy with the love of my life this time last year."

"What happened?" I'm almost afraid to ask, and he looks at me with a stricken expression. "She died, eight months ago."

"Richard, I'm so sorry." Reaching out, I instinctively grasp his hand to offer comfort, and he snatches it away as if I have the plague.

"I'm sorry Florence, even touching you felt like a betrayal. I can't do this."

The waiter arrives in the nick of time as Richard appears to fall into a full-blown panic attack.

As he drains yet another cocktail, I feel decidedly uncomfortable as he breaks down before my eyes.

"It was a car accident. Not her fault. She was cycling along the streets of London towards her office and got hit by a taxi. She died at the scene and I never even got to say goodbye."

"That's terrible, I'm so sorry."

He sniffs and blows his nose and says sadly. "I thought I could do this. My friends, family and everyone I know told me to move on and try to distance myself from the whole situation and I thought a cruise would do that. I feel as if I've just brought my problems with me though because they just won't go away."

"It's fine, you're grieving. Eight months is not that long and maybe you should just enjoy the break and not look for anything more."

I feel so sorry for Richard because who wouldn't. How is it that life can be all mapped out one minute and blown apart the next?

"Maybe, then again it may help to meet someone to distract me from my grief."

He slumps back in his seat. "Do you know how hard it is to pick up and carry on after losing the one you love? How can I look at the world the same way ever again? We had a future, marriage, babies and the house of our dreams and she should be on holiday with me, not dust already. How can fate be so cruel, Florence? Accidents are just a bad decision at the wrong time, a waste of a life and something that could have been avoided if she had just slept in late or taken a different route. How can a life be taken so cruelly when thieves, murderers and rapists live to old age? Belinda was so good, so loving and so amazing. She didn't deserve to die. I wish it was me."

I'm not sure what to say because whatever words make it out of my mouth won't be good enough. Poor Richard is still struggling and I'm not surprised and I'm almost certain I would feel the same in his position?

He looks at me with so much desperation I really want to make him feel better, but how? Instead, I just say sadly, "At least you have amazing memories of her. She will always live inside those and they will never change. My loss is easier to deal with but I'm still grieving a future I thought was all planned out."

"What do you mean?" Richard looks sympathetic and I sigh heavily. "I turned up at my wedding and discovered my groom had married someone else a few months before. As it happens, she was also at the wedding with his tongue down her throat while they waited for me to arrive."

Richard looks shocked, and I shrug. "Like you I'm grieving. Not for the man, but for the dream. For the future I thought I had coming and for the fact I need to start over again. I'm on my honeymoon with my bridesmaid and grasping at straws. Like you, it's too soon. I shouldn't be on this dating adventure; I should be taking care of Florence first. Maybe we should just accept that and move on with our lives, one step at a time until we are stronger. There's no sense in rushing something that may not be right for us. I'm sorry for your loss, Richard, at least yours is worth your grief."

"What do you mean?"

"I'm wasting time grieving for something that was never really mine in the first place. Oliver may have moved on already, but it's made me doubt my own mind. At least you know what you had was amazing. Cling onto it and cherish it because that will get you through, not a bad mistake wrapped up in a whole lot of regrets."

My phone buzzes in my pocket and I jump a little

because I'd almost forgotten I had set the alarm, notifying me about my date with Marcus.

Feeling like a complete fraud, I excuse myself, saying apologetically, "If you don't mind, I should meet my friend. Good luck and you'll be fine, we both will, we just need time to mend *us*."

He nods. "It was lovely to meet you, Florence. Maybe we could speak again, take those baby steps together."

"Possibly, anyway, enjoy your evening, I really should be going."

As I back away, I feel like a complete fraud as I leave one man in search of another. Maybe I should take my own advice and read a book or something because this cruise is turning out to be complicated in every way possible.

18

The Piano bar is located on the other side of the ship and it takes me ages to get there. I almost consider running but the heels I'm wearing won't allow that, so I power walk as quickly as I can.

All around me, people enjoy the luxuries this ship has to offer. More entertainment than you could ever imagine, shopping in tempting stores that are designed to ruin any cruise budget. Casinos, theatres, cinemas and even an ice rink. The good ship Aphrodite is a floating pleasure palace and yet here I am, charging around between men, looking for some form of connection because my last one was so cruelly severed.

I feel cut adrift and carried away by a wave of despair that I am struggling to surface from. Every decision I make it seems is the wrong one and threaten to pull me under and drown me. I must swim against the tide to stand any chance of survival, and so a tiny part of me really hopes that Marcus is about to throw me a lifeline.

∼

I SEE him as soon as I enter the piano bar and swallow hard. It's like a scene from a movie. Our eyes connect across the uncrowded room. He angles his chin and his eyes burn with an intensity that travels straight to my soul. He reels me in on the promise of more excitement than my body can stand and just seeing him dressed in a white dinner jacket like James Bond, makes me regret my hasty decision not to invite a man to my room because Marcus is definitely all man and I make my decision in a heartbeat. I want him to be *my* man.

He stands as I approach and I feel as if I'm walking on air. His dark gaze draws me to him and I physically ache to run my fingers through his dark silky hair.

His lips twitch, making me long to feel them attached to my own, and he reaches out as I near him and his hand grasps mine. Pulling me in, he kisses me three times on the cheek and I physically melt inside as I imagine being with a man like this.

"You look gorgeous." His voice is slightly husky, almost a whisper as he hovers close to my ear, and I feel a shiver pass through me as he pulls me to sit beside him in a booth that is hidden behind a pillar.

His leg presses against mine and I struggle to breathe because more than anything right now I want to discover what Marcus, drop dead gorgeous stranger, feels like.

"I have taken the liberty of ordering a bottle of champagne. I hope that's ok with you."

He pours me a glass from the ice bucket, and I seriously swoon.

"Lovely."

To my surprise, he reaches up and brushes a stray hair from my eyes and just feeling his fingers against my skin makes me hold my breath out of fear of disturbing a very welcome moment.

"So, this is nice."

I struggle to form words and he nods, a slow smile making his face relax a little.

"I've been looking forward to this all day."

Squirming a little on my seat, I try to drag my attention away from this gift from God and raise the glass to my lips and take a sip of the sparkling liquid. Unfortunately, it goes down the wrong way and for the next five minutes I cough as if I'm having an episode, ending up with Marcus having to thump my back several times in order for me to catch my breath. The fact I must be bright red with tears streaming down my face makes me feel absolutely mortified and only after I've got my breathing under control do I say weakly, "I'm sorry, that was embarrassing."

"Not really." He says with a smirk, "In my mind I just saved your life and now you owe me yours."

"What do you mean?"

I stare at him with complete devotion because he could tell me anything right now and I would believe every word.

He smiles and strokes my face lightly. "Your life belongs to me now. What am I going to do with it?"

His eyes flash wickedly and I don't even recognise myself right now because I have apparently become a spineless mess of lust and desire and he's only *looking* at me.

"I don't know. What *are* you going to do with it?" I can't stop flirting with him and my heart flutters as his mouth hovers dangerously close to mine and I lean in as if I'm desperate for a taste and he whispers, "I can think of several things I'd like to do but for now I have an offer you may want to consider."

"An offer?"

Anything, my body, my brain, definitely my body and my body. Did I mention that?

I can only think of one thing I want to give him right now and he says huskily, "Come and work for me, Florence, help me out with some properties I need to shift."

"Ok." I don't even ask how, where, how much and what my hours are. I would do anything for this man and he knows it, judging by the smirk on his face and the triumph in his eyes.

He starts to stroke my hand and I shiver inside as he says huskily, "Maybe we could conduct the training on board this ship. It would certainly save some time and when we return, I'll set up the appointments.

"To demonstrate the house?"

Despite everything, I am quite intrigued by this 'job' and look at him with curiosity. "Yes, I usually set up three a day and meet you there. I film and you perform, then when the house sells, I give you a percentage. So, you can see it's in your own interest to make the sales pitch count because then you earn more money."

It sounds almost too good to be true and I say quickly, "What about my friend, she would be interested too?"

"Great, but I'll need to interview her first. Maybe you could arrange a convenient time for that, say this time tomorrow, same place."

I feel a little put out that he will be enjoying a soiree with Sammy but understand the reasons behind it and just nod and smile rather flirtatiously. "Of course, I'll arrange it."

He looks at his watch. "Goodness, is that the time. I'm so sorry, Florence, I have another meeting to attend."

He slips a business card across the table towards me and says brightly, "My contacts. I'll look forward to working with you, and who knows, it may lead to other projects in the future. This could be the start of a beautiful friendship."

As he stands, he directs a look loaded with promises in

my direction and I feel a stirring of excitement inside that tells me I may be on the road to recovery already. Yes, Marcus is good for me because he's holding back, dangling the carrot in front of my eyes and making me interested in starting something that may restore my faith in men. If anyone can, he's that man. So as I watch him walk away, I feel hopeful for the future, which is more than I did just an hour ago.

I head back to our cabin/stateroom on a cloud of dizzy dreams and as expected, find it empty. Sammy is a little out-of-control right now and if I see her before 3 am, I'd be surprised. So, I make the most of my alone time and take a leisurely shower and pamper my body before grabbing a glass of champagne and heading out onto the balcony to gaze at the stars. As I lean against the rail, I'm surprised to discover that I'm ok. More than ok, actually. Life is full of opportunities that could pass by just as easily undiscovered if you let them.

Thinking back on my 'date' with Marcus, it strikes me how easy it would be to walk away from opportunity. If I'd never met him I would have passed by a new opportunity, possibly a new career, or even a better relationship. The *right* relationship. Maybe Oliver was a speed bump in the road and I was always meant to pass him by and I'm just grateful I found out sooner rather than later and if anything, I should be grateful to him for that.

As I sip my champagne, I offer a silent toast to myself. Here's to the future because I am so done with the past. My future looks bright and I will be in sole charge of making that happen.

Feeling optimistic for once, I even feel generous where it concerns Oliver, so I quickly type out a text to draw the line under my shattered relationship.

I take a selfie of me on the balcony with the glass of champagne held high in the air. Obviously, I apply a filter to make me look way better than I am and caption it.

Cheers to you and your new bride Grace. Thank you for setting me free. Strangely, I don't wish you were here because I am fast discovering I am better off without you. Have a nice life and enjoy married life while I get on with making mine way better than it would have been with you beside me.

Cheers, honey, thanks for everything. I learned a lot.

As I press send, I feel good about my life. Just thinking of Richard and his devastating experience makes me realise how short life is and not to waste a second of it. Yes, I've had a knock back but I'm starting to understand it just knocked some sense into me. If something's not right, deal with it and move on. I am and I'm more excited about that than anything.

19

Sammy groans as I shake her awake at 8am. "What time is it?" Her voice is slurred and sleepy and I note she is still fully dressed with her make-up smeared across the pillow.

"What time did you make it back here?" I stare at her with a mother's disapproval and she shrugs. "4am, why?"

"Please tell me you didn't end up in Tony's staff quarters or something."

"Tony?"

"Your date, the porter, remember."

"Oh yes, him." Sammy sits up and rubs her eyes, which only makes her look even more like a panda, and yawns loudly. "I should shower and change. I'm starving."

"Not before you tell me what happened."

She smiles with the excitement of someone who had the best night and says happily, "Tony cancelled, apparently he had to put in another shift and asked for a rain check."

"Probably for the best."

"Yes, it was ok. I was having too much fun with Dom to care."

"Dom?"

She grins. "My cruising in love date number two. He's amazing, Florrie. He was so much fun and is here with his brothers. I'm sure you'll meet some of them because they are also signed up to the programme. Anyway, he was good company, and we went dancing, drinking and ended up ice skating and I am definitely putting him to the top of my wish list when this ends."

I feel quite jealous of my friend and she looks at me sharply, "So, tell me about your two dates."

I fill her in, and she shakes her head sympathetically when I tell her about Richard. "Poor man, what a terrible thing to happen. You did the right thing though. I mean, you don't want the emotional baggage he brings with him. He obviously needs more time and we don't have that luxury because we are on a life mission with no time to waste."

"Apparently." I raise my eyes with disapproval, and she shrugs. "I'm single and free and determined to mingle. What's wrong with that?"

"Nothing. I just don't want you to make a reckless decision in the process. Anyway, tonight you have a meeting with Marcus to discuss a new career opportunity. Selling houses online. It could be the answer to your job worries."

She looks excited and says quickly, "Let me get ready, and you can fill me in over breakfast. I think I'm going for pancakes today with lots of syrup. Perfect."

She jumps out of bed and heads to the shower and as I reach for my phone, I notice a text from Oliver waiting to be read.

Feeling curious, I open it and stare at the message in disbelief.

Thanks for the text, Florrie, it's good to see you're having fun. Grace sends her love and says we must get together when you return and discuss the way forward. I'm glad there are no hard feelings, it wouldn't have worked anyway, I think we both know that. Sometimes things happen that are out of our control and maybe we were always meant to be friends. Enjoy your cruise, let me know how it goes because Grace and I are booked on a round the world one in January. Just a small favour though, please can you delete all pictures of us on your Facebook and Instagram feeds, it's just that Grace's family are friends of mine on Facebook and I don't want them to get the wrong idea when they see me pop up on your pages.

I feel slightly stunned as I stare at the message, as if I've misread it somehow. In less than one week Oliver is acting as if I was just a blip and plans to invite me around to tea or something. Friends – is he kidding me? And what was that about the photographs? Delete him from my newsfeed as quickly as he's deleted me from his life? I'm almost tempted to post every photo I ever took of us as a couple to flood my feeds, but that would make me look as if I'm pining after him.

It's as if I never knew him at all. He is like a stranger to me already, and it's only been a few days. What was that about being friends? As if I'm going to accept any cosy invitations to Sunday lunch and scroll through their holiday snaps. Oliver is in a bubble - in fantasyland if he thinks I will ever be ok with that.

If anything, I feel even more unloved, worthless and a mistake that everyone is happy he put right before it was too late.

Just thinking of him carrying on as if nothing has happened makes me feel so angry I almost can't think straight. I hear Sammy singing in the shower and for once think she's got the right idea. At least she's having fun. I'm struggling to accept I should move on with my life before the past one is even a distant memory.

I'm not sure if this is the moment I decide to change, but it certainly makes up my mind for me. I'm done with the old Florence Monroe. She's a doormat. Somebody who tries to do things the right way and considers that other people actually have feelings. Well, not anymore because my feelings count for more than the rest of them put together and I have the perfect opportunity to kick-start the new me. I'm on a love cruise and even if I don't find love at least I'll have a lot of fun trying.

∽

I FILL Sammy in over breakfast, and she looks excited.

"Wow, that sound amazing. So, if I've got this right, Marcus films us like we're some kind of virtual house presenter. We demonstrate a house and if it sells, we grab a percentage of the profits. That sounds like a piece of cake."

"I thought so too. He said he would train us on board this ship. I wonder what that involves?"

"I'm not sure." Sammy screws up her face as she thinks and then her eyes sparkle with excitement. "I actually can't wait, Florrie, because I've always known I have a gift for stardom."

"A gift for what - what on earth are you talking about?"

"Well..." She leans forward. "I've never told anyone this, but I went for an audition a few weeks ago for a television show."

"Why didn't you tell me?" I stare at her in amazement, and she shrugs. "To be honest, I was a little embarrassed because when I got there it wasn't something you'd want your friends and family to ever see."

"You mean..." My eyes are wide as she nods seriously. "Yes, it was that show where you stand behind a screen naked and someone decides whether they want to date you when they see your..." She whispers, "You know what."

"You were naked!"

The woman at the next table glares across at us, and Sammy giggles. "As the day I was born. Well, as it turned out, I wasn't picked, can you believe that? I wasn't sure whether to be relieved or annoyed. I mean, what's wrong with my private area? Just because I didn't have piercings in dodgy places, I was overlooked, probably for not being adventurous enough. Mind you, it was actually a good thing because the last thing I want is to discuss my television debut at coffee break the next day with my work colleagues after they saw me in all my naked glory."

"Then why did you do it, what if your gran, or even worse your dad saw you? How would he explain that down the pub?"

She shrugs. "I wore a wig and used a pseudonym."

"Wow, what name did you use?"

I'm not sure why, but she appears uncomfortable and looks around. "Well, enough about that. I really need seconds; I think I'll grab a bacon sandwich."

"Sammy...",

"What?"

"You used my name, didn't you?"

My heart sinks because I already know from her face that she did. For a moment I think she's going to tell me I've got it wrong, but instead she shrugs, looking guilty. "You don't mind, do you? I just said the first name that came into my head. At least it never aired, well, yet anyway."

"What do you mean *yet*?"

"Oh, I don't know, something about schedules and stuff, I wasn't really listening."

"But..." She heads off before I can speak and I stare after her, weighing up whether to rugby tackle her to the ground and threaten her with physical violence if she doesn't call them and withdraw her permission, or just do what I've always done and suck it up and hope for the best.

Feeling the new me rising to challenge her, I stop when I see the man she calls Danny grab her arm and pull her behind a display of fresh fruit.

Feeling curious, I quickly leave my seat and act as casually as possible as I pretend to be choosing between a display of watermelon or orange segments.

"I was jealous."

I can just make out Danny/Joseph's voice as he appears to be pleading with her.

"Not now, Joe."

"But last night..."

"Is none of your business."

"You should listen to me."

"Then maybe you should have taken your chance when it was on offer. I'm no longer that love-sick girl who hoped you would ask me out. I'm all grown up and capable of making my own decisions."

"But he's wrong for you, he's a player."

"Hm, takes one to know one..."

"Excuse me."

I jump guiltily as somebody obviously catches me eavesdropping and I see a woman glaring at me pointedly as I block everyone else from their five a day.

"Oh, I'm sorry." Quickly, I edge away and as I round the corner, I see Danny/Joe looking sadly after a retreating

Sammy Jo. He moves away before I make eye contact and I wonder what on earth is going on in my friend's life. She appears to be beating potential suitors off with a stick, and I'm so impressed right now. I am definitely going to have to up my game if I want to have half the fun she's obviously having and yet somehow my luck is nowhere near as good as hers appears to be.

I have yet to connect with any of my dates and Marcus, well, he may be unbearably hot, but something tells me he's as much a player as Joseph obviously was. Perhaps I'll have better luck today, surely third time lucky will make everything better.

20

Today's rendezvous is coffee and cake on the sundeck terrace and I see cruise ship Bobby, clipboard in hand, directing other single sailors to their port of call. A quick scan of the room shows many tables are taken already with couples who appear to be happy with their choices. I even see Richard chatting happily to a redhead who is laughing at something he is saying, and I feel happy for him. Maybe I caught him at a bad moment and he isn't as devastated as he appears to be.

Luckily, I don't see Norman anywhere which settles my nerves a little, although knowing him, he has found someone to help occupy his cabin and is enjoying a different kind of cake this morning.

Bobby grins as he sees me coming and consults his clipboard. "Welcome Florence, today is a good day for falling in love, wouldn't you agree?"

"Let's hope so, Bobby."

He looks across the terrace and points to a man sitting with his back to us. "There he is, Adam Peterson, your next date of interest."

He winks before stepping aside and saying brightly, "Go and get your man and failing that, the cake's good."

He winks as I head off, feeling quite nervous. From the back of him he looks normal. Short blonde hair and broad shoulders. It's difficult to tell really but I'm sure I'm overdue a bit of luck, so I plaster a smile on my face and stop by the side of the table.

"Um, hi, Adam, isn't it?"

He stands up and smiles and I relax a little. He seems nice, around my age, well-dressed and smells amazing.

"Hi, you must be Florence."

For some reason I look behind me, because it looks as if he's talking to someone else. Seeing nothing, I turn back and notice he's still looking past me and I say slowly, "Yes, um, that's me, Florence, but you can call me Florrie."

"Super. Let me pour you a cup of tea."

I sit opposite him and watch as his hands shake a little as he pours it and I feel a bit sorry for him. Obviously, he's nervous, and that's probably why he can't make eye contact.

He hands me the cup and I smile gratefully. "Thanks, the cake looks good."

There is a three-tier cake stand on the table between us and I see a feast of fruit cake, fairy cakes and lemon drizzle, not to mention some tiny macaroons.

"Yes, help yourself, I'm on a strict diet so they're all yours."

Not wasting a second more, I start loading my plate and he laughs. "You obviously like your food then."

"What do you mean?" I feel a little put out because what if he means I'm fat, greedy, or irresponsible?

"Sugar is worse than drugs if you ask me."

For some reason he is still talking to the imaginary guest behind me, and it's a little unnerving.

"Well, I do like cake. I mean, seriously, who doesn't and ordinarily I wouldn't get the opportunity to eat any but hey, I'm on holiday so I thought I'd take advantage of that."

He nods. "Yes, it's always the same. Give people a hall pass and they take advantage. Me, well I'm on a strict vegan, no dairy, protein diet where I only put enough fuel into my body to optimise its performance. For example, the calorie content of that fairy cake would take several days to work off. It would clog up your arteries and affect your body's ability to function. It's no wonder the government is taxing sugar left, right and centre and I heard salt is next. It's a good thing because the obesity crisis is even greater than the environmental one."

Placing my cake back on the plate, I have suddenly lost my appetite, as he says with some animation. "You know, I am starting a vegan warrior group and you're welcome to join if you like – in fact, you could be my first member. Well, other than me of course. I mean, it's early days and I've yet to recruit anyone."

Once again, I look behind me to see if there is actually another person he's talking to, but all I see is Sammy Jo feeding cake to a man who wouldn't look out of place in Heat Magazine.

My mouth drops as he returns the favour and looks deeply into her eyes and wipes a crumb from the side of her mouth with his thumb. Then he sucks it into his mouth, all the time staring at her with a look of pure, unbridled lust.

"So, Florence, what do you say, become my number one eco vegan and help me recruit others?"

Reluctantly, I turn back to my date who also appears to be looking at Sammy Jo, but who can tell, I'm not sure of anything anymore?

Feeling decidedly disgruntled at my sheer bad luck, I

disguise it well and say sadly, "I'm so sorry, I can't take you up on your offer."

"Why not?"

"Because well, um, I just adore meat, you know. In fact, I can't get enough of it. Yes, a lovely rare steak and what can I tell you about my desire for bacon every morning. Did I mention sausages?"

He looks past me in horror and I say wickedly. "You know, I could never give up meat. I love it too much. Vegetables are sooo boring, I would lose the will to live if that was my future. No, I'm sorry, meat all the way for this carnivore."

His look of disapproval should make me feel ashamed of myself, but I couldn't care less. The fact he's not even looking at me makes it easier because he is directing his disgust to someone behind me, anyway.

As I look around for an escape route, I catch the eye of a man at the next table and I swear my world stops still in a heartbeat.

This man is most definitely looking directly at me and suddenly I feel extremely hot indeed.

If you could picture David Beckham on a cruise, you wouldn't be far off and as his lips twitch as he listens shamelessly in on our conversation, I resist the urge to giggle.

Almost immediately he stands and my heart races to critical levels as he approaches our table and I openly drool at the sight of him as he stops and says in a husky voice, "Darling, there you are."

Adam looks up in surprise although this time he's looking in the other corner of the room as he says incredulously, "What's going on?"

Sexy stranger turns to him and says apologetically, "I'm so sorry, Florrie and I met yesterday and well, we got on rather well and promised to meet up today. She mentioned she had a meeting first and I'm sorry to interrupt but well, what can I say, I was keen to pick up where we left off."

"You know this man."

I try not to giggle as he looks past me again and it's like answering for someone behind me as I say apologetically, "I'm sorry, Adam, it's just that we met and discovered a shared love of MacDonald's. In fact, it was a close-run thing between that or KFC, both of which we are kind of addicted to."

Adam's lips thin and he stands rather abruptly and says tightly, "Then I'll bid you good day. It's obvious we are most unsuited so I won't waste any more of your time."

He heads off and sexy stranger Beckham slips into his seat and stares at me as I imagine I look when eyeing up a swiss roll.

"Thank you." I smile with relief, and he nods. "It was a pleasure."

"But how did you know my name?"

"I was listening in." He winks and offers me his hand across the table. "Jake Hudson at your service."

"Florence Monroe."

He clasps my hand tightly, and I almost melt into a puddle of lust and gratitude. At last, God has answered my prayers.

"I'm sorry to ruin your date but by the looks of it you needed rescuing."

"Was it that obvious?"

"Just a little."

He looks at the cake stand and grins. "Well, it would be a shame to waste these delightful delicacies. Allow me."

He spears a small piece of lemon drizzle cake onto a fork and holds it tantalisingly close to my lips, and I shamelessly allow him to feed me.

As my lips close around the fork, I almost groan with happiness and for a moment must close my eyes because when I open them, he is smiling. "You like."

"Do you really have to ask?"

I watch, almost panting as he eats some of it himself, and then stops a passing waitress who almost skids to a halt bedside him.

"Yes, sir." From the look in her eyes, he is having the same effect on her and from the look in his he's used to it because he just says politely, "Please may I order a fresh pot of tea and some cups?"

"Yes, sir, anything else – at all."

He shakes his head. "No, that's all for now."

He turns his attention back to me and the look he gives me would melt the sun and I shiver with so much excitement I'm surprised it doesn't rock the ship. This is it, my reward for everything that has happened in my life that went wrong, all rolled up into one right package of perfection with my name on a gift tag around his neck.

21

I'm trying so hard to act cool, but after the run of bad luck I've had I'm failing miserably. He is the first decent guy to head my way, and I need to step up and make this count.

He looks at me as if I'm the most interesting person in the world and smiles.

"So, Florence, tell me about yourself. What's your story?"

"Well..." I stop and think because I need to pluck a leaf from Sammy's book and make myself appear interesting and not some jilted bride with no other options, so I smile with what I hope is a mysterious air and lean back in my chair.

"I'm a beautician by trade. I have my own business that does rather well."

"I'm impressed, although you look the sort."

"What's that supposed to mean?"

"Beautiful."

"Oh." I'm not sure what else to say and just giggle nervously that immediately makes me look like an idiot and so I quickly say, "What do you do, as an occupation?"

"Computers. IT for an insurance company. It's boring but keeps me in beers at the weekend so I can't complain."

"Any, um, girlfriends, a wife perhaps?"

I actually hate myself right now as I quickly ask the only question I want answered.

"Not yet."

He winks and pops a piece of walnut and coffee cake in his mouth and chews slowly and I am almost salivating right now as I watch the poor man eat, and it's not because of the food. Trying to focus my mind on my manners instead, I say brightly, "So, this is all rather strange, isn't it?"

He nods. "Yes, you could say that. I expect you're another member of this weird cruising in love thing. I guessed as much by your rather strange cake date."

"To be honest, this whole thing is a disaster, for me anyway. However, my friend over there is living her best life right now."

I wave in Sammy's direction and he laughs softly, "She's your friend, interesting."

"Why?" Suddenly I'm a little worried about what sort of reputation Sammy has earned herself already judging by the laughter in his eyes and he leans forward and whispers, "She was out with Dom last night and now it's apparently Brad's turn."

"They're your friends?"

He nods. "Brothers actually. Unfortunately, we got to holiday together this year, not by choice but it's been ok. Anyway, your friend is such good fun and Dom was quite taken with her, but according to the rules of the club we have to date a different girl every day for a week. One thing's for sure, your friend will have quite a decision to make at the end of it because they're lining up to win a week with her and are all trying to outdo each other."

I stare across at Sammy in shock and see her laughing at something this Brad guy is saying. He is looking at her as if she's his one true love and feel a pang of envy for my lucky friend.

"So, tell me about your dates so far. Anyone interesting?"

"What…?" I shake my head as he pulls my attention back to him and then feel cheated when I think of my own experiences.

"They've not been so great, actually. First one up was old enough to be my grandad and wanted me to keep him company in his cabin."

Jake looks shocked and then raises his eyes. "And you weren't tempted – what's wrong with you?"

He laughs again, and I shiver with disgust. "It was quite traumatic, really. I had to report him because he could be some kind of sex pest or something and they need to know."

"Aren't we all?"

"What?"

"Sex pests."

"I sincerely hope not."

I stare at him in horror as my dream of happy ever after comes close to becoming happy ever disaster again and Jake laughs. "It's what my first date called me."

"Why?" Once again, I feel my walls go up as he rakes his fingers through his hair and grins.

"Her name was Gail, and she works as a secretary. I think she was in her thirties, but looked much older. Not a grandma though, I suppose I was lucky there."

I roll my eyes as he laughs. "Anyway, she spent the whole time telling me how much she hated men. The men in her office who were only after one thing. The managers who undressed her with their eyes at the morning meeting. The customers who flirted openly with her on the phone and, quite frankly, any male that ever breathed the same air as her. Well, it made me wonder why she was looking for love on a cruise and she glared at me and told me that she wasn't getting any younger and her eggs were fast approaching their sell by date. She was looking for a man to impregnate her – her words – so she could have a family before her shelf life expired."

"Oh dear." My lips twitch as he pulls a face. "Well, needless to say, I made my excuses and left because quite frankly she scared the hell out of me."

Despite myself I can't stop laughing and he pulls a face and says with mock pain, "Then there was Faye, who seemed nice enough but had so much Botox she appeared permanently surprised. Her mouth was fixed into a weird pout and I couldn't make out what she was trying to say because her lips hardly moved. She had so much make-up on I couldn't tell you how old she was and she had absolutely zero conversation and it was quite hard going. At the end of it I couldn't get out of there fast enough and she seemed upset when I declined her invitation to join her for a couple's massage. Anyway, tell me about your next date, surely that one was better."

This time I lower my voice because Richard isn't that far away and leaning forward, say furtively, "He's over there, talking to that redhead."

Jake looks and I hiss, "Don't look, he'll know I'm talking about him."

"Hardly. He can't take his eyes off his date. That may be a match made in heaven by the looks of it."

"I hope so, because his girlfriend died not long ago, and he's finding it hard. He completely broke down when I asked if he had anyone and I spent the rest of the date consoling him. It was sad and yet rather exhausting and after the date you rescued me from, I'm seriously thinking of quitting the programme, it's obviously not in my best interest."

"I didn't have you down as a quitter, Florence?"

"Then prepare to be shocked because not only may I quit this programme, I also quit my wedding."

He looks surprised, and I nod miserably. "It turns out my groom was already married and his wife was a guest at my wedding to her husband."

"Are you kidding me?"

Jake looks absolutely horrified, and I nod vigorously. "To be honest, it was a miracle in disguise because I was having doubts, anyway. It's obvious we weren't suited, and he did me a favour, really. So, I jilted him at the altar due to the fact he was making out with his wife while they waited for me, in full view of my family and friends. I'm not really sure what they were planning. I mean, maybe she was going to stand up and be that person who knows a good reason why the bride and groom shouldn't be married. Perhaps he was going to let it go that far, which shows how spineless he was, anyway."

Jake looks a little uncomfortable and probably thinks I'm a maniac, and I sigh heavily.

"Well, it was a blessing in disguise and I left them to it and here I am now. My past far behind me and my future uncertain but not unwelcome."

It suddenly strikes me that he was surely meant to be meeting a date of his own.

"Anyway, why were you alone, did your date not show?"

"Food poisoning, apparently. Bobby told me to wait and he would see what he could do. It was fine though, apparently her name was Deidre, and she was some kind of crochet champion, whatever that is."

"Crochet, or croquet?"

"One of them. Do you know what on earth either of them is?"

"Of course. I know a lot of useless information. In fact, I'm the queen of it and crochet is some kind of knitting thing and croquet is a game where you hit a ball with a mallet through a hoop. It sounds right up my street the way I'm feeling after the last date. I mean, did he strike you as odd, he couldn't even look me in the eye?"

Jake starts laughing, and I stare at him in amazement. "What's so funny?"

"You are."

"Why, what have I said?"

"Your date was looking directly at you."

"No he wasn't."

"He was, at least he thought he was. He has a lazy eye, something he can't help. I'm surprised a woman who knows useless information didn't know that."

"I said *useless*, not *useful*. Gosh, if I had known he was afflicted, I would have been more sympathetic. I feel like a bitch."

Jake laughs and as I watch his eyes twinkle, it strikes me just how good looking he is. He is obviously a player because anyone who looks like David Beckham must have a string of women, and some men, lining up at his door.

Bobby chooses this moment to stop by our table and wags his finger at us both.

"Naughty, naughty, you have indulged in some unauthorised partner swapping. You have seriously messed with my programme, you know. I'm going to mark this as both your dates and place Adam with Faye as no shows." He sighs and drums his pencil on his clipboard impatiently.

"It's not easy playing cupid you know. We're not even a

third of the way through and my stress levels are causing my eczema to flare up. The sooner we reach week two the better."

He looks across at Sammy, who appears to be choking with laughter and his face softens. "Now there's a girl who knows how to play the game to the max. So far every date I've sent her on has requested her as their final match. They haven't even waited to meet the others. What can I say, that woman is a legend."

Jake catches my eye and grins as Bobby heads across to Sammy's table to heap even more praise on her over-inflated ego.

"You're so jealous."

Jake's voice reminds me I must be staring at her with a look of envy and I say quickly, "No, I'm not. I'm pleased for her."

"It's written all over your face. There's no need though."

"I know there's no need because I'm not jealous." I stare at him with a firm expression, and he shrugs. "You needn't be. Brad's only doing this to wind Dom up."

"Why?"

"Because he's always so smug. He always gets the girl and thinks no sane female can resist him. We thought we'd teach him a lesson and cut him down to size. It's just a bit of fun but we'll back off when it comes to it."

"We?"

"Well, Brad. I'm more interested in her friend."

For some reason his words shock me into silence and a warm delicious feeling passes through me as he stares at me with those gorgeous velvet brown eyes that dance with desire. It's not unwelcome and I feel myself blush a little as he says in a whisper, "Would you like to grab some sea air? We could continue our conversation outside."

I don't even need to think about it and nod. "Ok, that sounds good."

I'm not sure why but as we stand to leave the safety of the cake table, it feels as if I'm about to take a step into the unknown and it's so strange to be walking with another man by my side who isn't Oliver. Not that I'm complaining because as upgrades go, this one exceeds all expectations and something tells me that this moment is one I will never forget.

22

It feels good walking beside Jake and I don't miss the envious looks that are thrown my way as we meander through the tables laden with more cake than a bake-off competition.

As we venture outside, the sun hits me and for the first time this trip, I feel warm, happy and hopeful for the future.

"So, what do you fancy doing?"

A million things immediately come to mind but I settle for, "Shall we grab a couple of sun beds and people watch?"

"Sounds good."

We head down to the main deck and due to the weather it's impossibly crowded and if there is even one solitary sun bed, we would be lucky.

"Maybe we need a Plan B." Jake sighs.

I nod. "Maybe we should try one of the quieter areas. You know, for a ship this size it can appear crowded sometimes. There must be somewhere that's not so busy, surely."

As we walk, I probe a little to find out more about my interesting companion.

"So, you say you're on holiday with your brothers. Do you usually holiday together?"

"Not normally, but this was a special occasion."

"That sounds interesting. What is it, a special birthday perhaps or a celebration?"

"None of the above. If you must know…"

For some reason he sounds a little sad and I prepare myself to discover the weird reason this guy is still single at all and apparently interested in me.

"Our father died."

He sounds upset as his voice shakes, and I'm unsure what to say because I wasn't expecting that.

I settle for a sympathetic, "I'm so sorry, Jake, that's terrible."

"Yes – it is."

For a moment we wander aimlessly along and I don't know what to do. Should I rub his arm to show I'm here for him, or just let him have a moment and stay silent? Then he says brightly, "Anyway, we don't need to speak about that right now. Let's talk about you and where you go from here. I mean, from the sounds of it you haven't had a lot of luck yourself lately."

Thinking about Oliver probably cosying up to his wife as we speak, I beg to differ because luck is apparently what I have an abundance of. "To be honest, Jake, it's fine, you see luck is very much on my side right now because if I hadn't found out about Oliver and his wife and his shaky morals, I would be married to him right now – illegally I might add and have the whole nightmare to deal with. Instead, I am on a Caribbean cruise heading for the British Virgin Islands, entertaining endless men on fascinating dates, most of which are showing me why I really should stay single for my own protection."

"Most of them."

"All of them actually."

He staggers as if I've wounded him and I smirk. "You, of course, are excluded from that because you are not my official date. You are my rescuer, of which I will be eternally grateful."

"So, if I asked you out on a date, what would it be? I mean, there are endless activities to choose from on board and if you could do anything right now, what would you choose?"

"I'm not sure, what's the choice?"

He pulls out his phone and scrolls to a page before handing it over.

As I look at the screen, a million things to do dance before my eyes and I say with considered interest, "Well, I could watch you in the world's sexiest man competition, that's quite some title to earn. You'd have stiff competition, mind; this ship is a hotbed of potential contenders for that title and I'm guessing Adam is already oiling up as we speak."

"Interesting. Do you like that sort of thing?"

"Obviously not. Why would I be interested in staring at a group of hot guys flexing their abs and pouring hot oil on their bodies?"

I grin as he rolls his eyes and I consult the list. "There's a table tennis competition that could be good but would involve me revealing I can't actually hit anything but fresh air, so that may not work. There's an interesting seminar on discovering your inner zen that I could probably use right now, or the pathway to Yoga looks fun."

He retrieves the phone and just feeling his fingers brush against mine, makes me shiver a little and reminds me just how handsome this man is, making me believe in miracles right now because why on earth is this man still single? There must be a reason, unless he isn't and has a girlfriend or wife stashed away at home looking after their children.

"What about balloon artistry, I could make you a dog hat?"

"Could be fun. What else have you got?"

I peer over his shoulder and he edges a little closer.

"Well, there's an afternoon guitar melody that sounds like a whole heap of fun, or the senior facelifts afternoon day spa, that could be beneficial."

"Show me that, you are kidding, surely."

Staring at the screen, I see that he's not and say in wonder, "Wow, this ship has everything. I wonder if I should tell Ellen about that."

"Who's Ellen?"

"A rather interesting woman I met who is here with her third husband, I believe. They met on board another ship and it gave me hope that all is not lost."

"Good for them. Anyway, I have made my decision and as I made it first, you get to choose the next activity."

Feeling strangely happy that we have a second activity already lined up, I fall into step beside him and follow him to what I seriously hope is a nice romantic, intimate, proper date.

~

"You really thought this was the best thing on offer."

He laughs as he sits opposite me with an eager woman staring at his muscles a little too closely, and I swear I see saliva pooling at the corner of her mouth.

In fact, I am having a hard time distracting my own

attention away from his rock-hard biceps and concentrating on my own humiliation right now.

"Don't you like yours then?"

"I haven't seen it yet."

The woman attending my own arm says brightly, "I think it's a good choice, sir."

She would. I'm betting anyone human would think anything this man says and does is the right thing, oh to be drop dead gorgeous and super sexy, it certainly gets you far in life.

He strains to look at his arm, and I giggle. "No peeking."

"I'm not, I'm just mildly curious what you chose."

"It will be fine, trust me."

"Why don't I then?"

The girl hanging off his arm winks at me, making me warm towards her a little more.

My own master artist sighs and pats my arm, before saying with a hint of envy, "There, you're all done."

She hands me a mirror and I glance across at Jake, who is smirking and I almost dread looking. As I raise the mirror to look at my arm, I expect to see a picture of a cute kitten or something, instead I see a red love heart with three words etched on my skin.

Property of Jake

"Oh my God." I stare at it in horror as the words swim before my eyes. "Why?"

He laughs out loud and part of me loves every minute of the envy in both girl's eyes.

"To tell your other dates that you have met your match already and to back off."

"Have I though because if you're referring to Norman, Richard or Adam, your choice sucks."

"I think the name gives away the identity, anyway, now it's my turn."

The girl beside him pats his arm a little longer than strictly necessary and I don't blame her one bit and I giggle as he takes the mirror and laughs out loud. "Classic."

"Do you like it?"

"Strangely, I do."

The women look at him with even more adoration as he looks proudly at his tattoo of Tinkerbell fluttering on his sexy bicep.

He smiles across at me and I swear my legs lose all feeling as I turn to a puddle of lust and desire.

"So, now we are joined by ink, let's go and celebrate."

Thanking the two women who take one last lingering look at my 'date' and I'm surprised but not upset when he reaches for my hand and pulls me up before leaning down and whispering, "You're mine now, it's written in ink as a permanent reminder."

"Until I shower, of course."

"No, for the rest of eternity."

Why does that make me happy? I've obviously had too much sun and as I walk beside him, still clutching his hand, I offer a prayer of thanks to the goddess Aphrodite because she has excelled herself this time.

23

It feels like ages since I saw Sammy Jo, so it's with some relief we manage to grab an hour of sunbathing before changing for dinner. I have to admit she looks amazing in a vibrant blue bikini and judging by the number of selfies she's taking; she's sharing them with her adoring followers on Instagram. As I watch, it reminds me of how much I always envied her. She has always been a free spirit, seemingly unconcerned about anything in life. Most people agonise over every decision they make, not her. She has always rolled with the punches and it obviously makes her happy.

Even at school when the rest of us spent sleepless nights studying for our exams, she got her full eight hours and rocked up with a full face of makeup and tales of the interesting date she had the night before – to distract her from the day ahead. We all thought she would fail and some hoped that was the case because where we worked tirelessly to scrape through, Sammy Jo always walked away with A*s.

It was surprising when she decided to forego college and

start work at the local factory. She could have done anything, but she wasn't interested in pursuing anything academic. She has always been more interested in enjoying life and having 'experiences' and always said she'd grow up when it was time.

The fact she no longer has a job would have most people surfing job sites and setting up interviews, but not Sammy Jo. She's more interested in working on her tan.

I envy her that luxury because I've always been one who burns easily and needs to sit in partial shade with factor 50 as a minimum.

She stretches out beside me as she draws some admiring glances from a couple of men who pass by and as she leans on her front, she sighs, "You know, Florrie, I could get used to this life. I need to find a rich man to indulge my new passion of travel."

"Why a man, find something you're good at and earn enough money yourself?"

"I need a man for what I'm good at."

She winks and despite myself I grin because Sammy Jo could charm a priest. She is so adorable.

"So, tell me about my meeting later with the estate agent. What do I need to know?"

I had almost forgotten about Marcus and that alone shocks me because this morning he occupied most of my thoughts.

"Well, I think he just needs to see if you're good in front of the camera. You know, personable and at ease with performing."

"Got it."

She looks out to sea and sighs. "You know, I'm so grateful that Oliver broke your heart and crushed your dreams because it's given me this golden opportunity I would never have had. There's always a silver lining you know."

"Great, I'm glad my personal trauma is so pleasing to you."

I laugh because actually Oliver is so far from my mind I should be worried about my morality because I appear to have replaced him rather too quickly for decency and I should question that.

"So, tell me about your dates. I saw you were with Brad's brother Jake, he looked nice."

"He is."

I flash her my arm that has been so modestly covered by a sarong and she shrieks with laughter. "A tattoo, that's amazing, I want one."

"It's not a permanent one, only airbrushed on. Could you imagine if it was, how would I explain that to my parents?"

We giggle, and then she looks at it thoughtfully. "So, I'm guessing he chose that. What did you choose for him?"

"Tinkerbell."

"Good choice. So, what happens now, are you going to mark him as your number one?"

For a moment I forgot about the stupid singles programme and nod. "Yes, to be honest, I doubt I'll bother with anyone else. It's all been more miss than hit with me. What about you?"

"I'm hitting perfect tens every time. My only problem is choosing which one I prefer. Do you think I could set up one of those reverse harem situations, that would be cool?"

If I thought she was joking I would laugh but knowing my friend she means every word, so I say carefully, "Your life is not a sleazy romance novel, Sammy Jo, and you should really change your preferences. No, you will not offer that up as your decision to cruise ship Bobby and choose the one you want to spend the most time with. Anyway, they may not choose you. Have you thought of that?"

I feel like knocking her down a little because it annoys me slightly that she is winning at this where I am enjoying a rather bumpy road to love.

"Keep telling yourself that Florrie because cruise ship Bobby's already told me I'm the front runner with every date so far, so I should really be generous and share myself wouldn't you agree?"

She laughs as I roll my eyes and then lowers her voice.

"Seriously though, I am having such a good time I will probably send Oliver and Grace a Christmas card every year for the rest of my life, but…"

"What?"

Suddenly, the atmosphere changes and she sighs. "I caught sight of Joseph when I was on my date with Brad. He was with someone."

"What, a cruising in love cake date?"

"No, I saw him out of the window on a sun bed next to a glamorous brunette who looks nothing like me. He was rubbing suntan lotion on her back and if they aren't lovers, I'm not enjoying the biggest ego trip a girl can ever experience."

"Does it bother you?"

"It did a bit. I suppose I always think of Joseph as unfinished business and the one that got away. It hurts me a little to know that I never measured up and I know it's silly but it's a part of my life I never drew a line under and seeing him here brings it all back. Do you think he's on his honeymoon, or a sexy holiday with the girl of his dreams?"

Thinking of her conversation with him at breakfast, I wonder if she's had words already and say carefully, "I overheard you talking to him earlier. What was that all about?"

"I'm not sure, really. He pulled me aside and told me he saw me with Dom the other night and I should steer clear of him."

"Bloody cheek, what business is it of his?"

"Exactly. He made out he was concerned, making me think he wanted more, but when I saw him with that woman, I realised he'd never changed. He's still keeping his balls in the air and hedging his bets and I'm better off without him."

"But what if it was always meant to be him, and what did he mean, warning you away from Dom?"

I get an uncomfortable feeling inside because Jake's words come back to me when he told me Dom was interested and his brother Brad was playing with her. Has Sammy Jo been caught up in a mad game of deception and why is Joseph so concerned, anyway?

I feel a headache coming on, and Sammy sighs. "Maybe I need a night off from men. How about, after my meeting with Marcus, we catch a show or go ice skating? I'll tell Dom I can't meet him for cocktails in the Moon bar."

"You've got another date with him, isn't that against the rules?"

"Probably, but I never follow them, anyway. I've still got four more prospects lined up and I'm exhausted already. Maybe I should just take a regenerating nap and wake up a lot wiser."

She turns over and I envy her ability to switch off and power nap. My mind is buzzing with everything that's happened in such a short space of time and if I was her, I would be an anxiety ridden mess right now. How have we both managed to mess up our lives inside a week? At least I still have my job I suppose, but even that has lost its shine a little. Maybe we should both take Marcus up on his job offer and start again. Surely, we can't make a mess of it the second time around.

24

Tonight we ate in the Grill house restaurant and it was a pleasant change from the main dining room. The steak was seriously good, and it wasn't as crowded as the usual one, which took the tempo down a little and we enjoyed a lovely evening of girly chat and a bottle of wine.

As we polish off two crème brûlées with crème anglaise, it's lovely to see Ellen and Geoffrey who stop by our table on their way to their own.

"Darlings, it's been ages since Mamma Mia. How are things? Have you met the man of your dreams yet?"

"Men, actually." Sammy Jo looks smug and Ellen claps her hands with joy.

"Super darling, you must tell me all about them."

Geoffrey looks a little disgruntled and moans, "I'm hungry, can't you hear about it later?"

"No Geoffrey, we have plans, remember."

Ellen winks at me and I feel a giggle coming on as Geoffrey turns a little red and mumbles, "I'll see you at the table."

"What was that all about, what are your plans?" Sammy looks interested, and Ellen lowers her voice.

"Well, we've got an activity planned that we both enjoy a little too much. Strictly invite only, and if I told you what it was, I would have to kill you. One word of advice, darlings, never stop living life, no matter how old you are because your body may age but your mind never does. Don't be held back by what you think you should be doing, do whatever your heart desires and to hell with what's right."

Once again, she winks and heads off, and Sammy whistles. "Wow, my money's on some kind of naughtiness below decks. Way to go, Ellen, when I grow up, I want to be just like her."

"Sammy Jo Miles, wash your mouth out, as if Ellen would be bothered with all that."

"I'm not so sure. I'm guessing Ellen is a bit of a dark horse and underneath that respectable clothing is a wicked wanton woman fooling the world into thinking she's respectable."

"Well, if she is, good luck to her."

The waiter stops by our table and smiles at Sammy, who has flirted outrageously with him the entire meal, resulting in an invitation to the staff disco tomorrow night on the employees only deck.

"Can I get you anything else, ladies?"

He includes us both but only has eyes for Sammy and she smiles. "No thanks, Ben, you've been a rock star, thanks for such a great evening."

"The pleasure was all mine."

Once again, he looks lustfully at my man magnet friend, and I cough awkwardly. "Anyway, it's um, just before eight, haven't you got a meeting to attend?"

Sammy jumps up quickly. "Goodness, is it that time

already? Can you believe I've got a job interview, Ben? There's never any rest for the wicked you know."

"On the ship, that's amazing. I'll act as a reference for you if you like and show you around."

"No, sadly not on the ship but if you hear of anything going, let me know."

She grins at the crestfallen waiter and we head off to the Piano bar where Marcus will be waiting.

Just thinking of the delectable Marcus conflicts me a little because he is so good looking, so mysterious and so desirable, I'm not sure I want Sammy Jo to meet him at all but she needs a job and he's offering and it would be churlish of me to stand in the way of that.

As we enter the bar, I point him out as he waits, studying his phone at the same table as before.

"Wow, Florrie he is something else. Thanks for this."

"You're welcome. I'll, um wait in the Moon bar, good luck."

She nods with excitement and heads his way, and I shamelessly linger in the shadows to watch his reaction to her.

My heart sinks when he stands and looks her over appreciatively before guiding her to the seat opposite and pulling out her chair.

For the first time, I notice a smile on his lips and a spark in his eyes that makes my heart sink. Of course he likes her. They all do. Why wouldn't they?

Sammy Jo is every man's dream, apparently. A blue-eyed blonde with curves in all the right places. A figure like a Victoria Secrets model and a quick wit and engaging conversation. She is smart, sexy and fun and I'm an idiot for making her my best friend because with her around, I always fall into the role of wing woman.

"Hey gorgeous."

A husky voice whispers behind me and I spin around to see Jake leaning on the wall, watching me with an amused grin.

"Spying on people now; caught red handed."

"For your information..." I stand a little taller and make my expression one of boredom.

"I was introducing my friend, you know the one all the guys apparently want, to a man who only wants her for her job skills."

"Are you sure about that?"

"What?"

"Well, from where I'm standing that man is not thinking about any old job offer right now."

Spinning around, I see Sammy Jo laughing at something Marcus is saying, and for some reason they are holding hands. I stare at them in disbelief because it's only been two minutes. What the hell?

Jake laughs. "This ship is full of surprises. I never thought I'd see that man crack a smile; your friend is a skilful player; he may have just met his match."

"She's *not* a player, and what do you mean, do you know that man?"

"Sadly, yes I do. He's my older brother Marcus."

"Your what?"

I stare at him in complete surprise, and he nods.

"Yes, I told you I was on this trip with my brothers. Three of them, actually. Dom, Brad and Marcus."

If I wasn't so shocked, I'd be impressed because there are some amazing family genes in these guys. Their parents must have been film stars or something.

I feel so confused and Jake obviously senses that and steers me away from the bar and out onto the deck.

"You must be wondering what's going on right now."

"A little. I mean, you told me you were on holiday with your brothers but I'm starting to sense something's not quite right. Sammy Jo appears to be in huge demand with your family and I'm wondering why?"

"They may all have the same type, haven't you thought about that?"

"Not really. Maybe you should explain what you meant when you told me your other brother was only giving her attention to wind your brother Dom up. What's the purpose of that because if my friend is going to get hurt in the process, I am not ok with that."

Jake runs his fingers through his hair and looks a little troubled. He appears to be weighing up whether to tell me something and after a while, sighs heavily.

"Ok I'll tell you but you mustn't breathe a word of this to anyone and definitely not your friend."

"I can't promise that. What if she's in danger, I'd definitely tell her then?"

He laughs out loud, making me feel a little foolish.

"Your friend is most definitely not in danger and if anything has an exciting proposition heading her way."

We set off, and it strikes me how lucky I am to be here. It's like a mini city on the water as we pass bars, clubs and theatres. There is something for everyone and almost too much to do. Having been at sea for two days, I am looking forward to reaching dry land tomorrow and I hope Sammy is happy to still explore with me.

Jake is an easy companion to walk beside. Good looking, funny and attentive. The trouble is, he's almost too perfect and there are several red flags waving me on, warning me to guard my heart at all costs because it's in extreme danger right now.

Trying hard to keep any feelings I have to myself, I walk with Jake to one of the lounges where they are serving coffee, and I'm grateful for the soft settees set around little tables that make it feel more relaxing somehow.

Jake sits beside me and it feels good as he drapes his arm nonchalantly across the back of the sofa and to anyone watching, we could be any other couple on board.

We order a couple of cappuccinos and while we wait, Jake says in a low voice.

"Remember I told you my father died." He sighs. "Well, it wasn't unexpected because he had been ill for some time. He was lucky to survive as long as he did, which as it turns out, wasn't in our best interests."

"Why, what did he do?"

I am riveted because from the look on his face, it's not a happy tale.

"Well, my father was a self-made man who built up a successful company from scratch. Building supplies mainly with a chain of outlets across the country and he always wanted us to follow him into the family business but we had other ideas."

"He must have been upset."

"He was, which is why he used his time wisely when he learned he didn't have much of it left. When the will was read we thought it would go to our mum. It's best that way and she needed to be provided for and she was to a point."

"He cut her out, that's horrible."

Jake laughs. "Not entirely. She still has more money than she will ever spend and gets to remain in the family home as long as she wants to. There's a coach house in the grounds she has decided to renovate and is planning on moving into it early next year."

"So, what happens to the company and the main house, do you all get to share it or something?"

"Not exactly." He seems worried about telling me and I feel bad for that, but I need to know that Sammy Jo isn't being set up in something that will break her heart.

He carries on. "The will was read, and the outcome is the reason we are on this cruise - not by choice, I might add."

"Why, what's wrong with it?"

"Nothing if you're older. I suppose if you are here with someone you love it would be ok but it's not really our thing."

"What is then?"

"Skiing, scuba diving, white water rafting and partying. Sunning ourselves on a super yacht, you know, standard things to do on holiday."

Thinking of my own holidays that usually involve sunbathing religiously in Spain and partying at night, I can't possibly imagine the sort of life Jake lives.

"So, here we are with one aim in mind. To meet someone and fast."

"I'm confused. Why do you need to meet someone because your dad died?"

The coffee arrives at the punchline and I feel so frustrated I almost consider waving the waiter away and by the time we've sorted out who's having what and how many sugars, I am so frustrated. It's like getting to the end of the whodunnit and the page is missing.

Jake grins ruefully. "Before I tell you, you need to know this has nothing to do with why I am keen on spending time with you. I am not part of this charade, just an amused bystander loving watching his brothers fight for what they want the most."

"Sammy Jo."

"No, their inheritance."

Now I am so confused and decide to let him speak with no interruptions because I think I'm complicating things.

He looks worried. "Florence, remember this is between me and you and doesn't concern us in any way. Your friend will be fine because my brothers may be desperate but they're not total idiots."

"Are you saying they're only after Sammy Jo because they're desperate?"

I feel so annoyed for her and Jake laughs.

"I'm not saying that at all. Like I said, Dom really likes her and not just because of what she can give him."

"Are you talking about sex because if you are, she's not that kind of girl? In fact, neither am I just in case you were wondering."

My cheeks blush as I speak, probably due to the lies rolling off my tongue with delusional ease. Sammy Jo is definitely like that and I would be too if it concerned a night with him, but I don't need him to know that.

To my surprise, he takes my hand and squeezes it before saying sweetly, 'I'm glad to hear that, it's refreshing in this day and age."

"Are you saying I'm old-fashioned now?"

I grin as he laughs and shakes his head, lifting my hand to his mouth and kissing it softly.

"Maybe I'm the old-fashioned one. Perhaps I'm not that kind of guy either."

Now my hopes are dashed and I'm screaming inside. Just my luck to attract a gentleman. Why is fate so cruel?

"So..." he sighs heavily. "The reason we are here is to find a woman, someone to take home and..."

"What?"

"Marry."

For a moment it doesn't really sink in, and I just stare at him in confusion. He sips his coffee and watches me for my reaction, and yet I don't think I have one. I'm numb and in a weird daze because why does everything in life lately revolve around a wedding deception?

I'm not sure how I feel about it and my face must fall because he says with concern, "I'm sorry, I've shocked you."

"You have."

He shifts a little beside me and sighs. "I thought it would, it's crazy, isn't it?"

"But why?"

"Because my dad was fed up with us playing the field and fooling around. He wanted us to grow up and face our responsibilities, so in order to lay our hand on our inheritance, we need to be married. If we divorce within two years, we get nothing. If we have children inside of two years, we get it all immediately."

"Hang on a minute.

I stare at him in shock. "Are you seriously telling me that your brothers, one of them anyway, want to impregnate my friend for money. That's disgusting."

"It depends how you look at it."

His eyes twinkle, and I shove him hard. "You know it's disgusting; as if Sammy's womb is for sale."

Once again I'm telling myself that more than him because knowing my friend, she would think it was some kind of super adventure and be definitely up for it.

Jake nods. "Anyway, like I said, it has nothing to do with me because I'm not interested in any of it."

"Why not?"

Maybe he's a super billionaire already and doesn't need it. I've heard of stranger things and he is in IT, after all.

There's Bill Gates, that Facebook guy and the one in Two and a Half Men and Ashton Kutcher is definitely my kind of billionaire.

"I'm happy as I am. I make enough to get by. I don't want to run my father's business and I like living in town. The last thing I want is a hasty wedding to someone I will be cutting out of my life quicker than I persuaded them to be there in the first place."

"But I still don't understand where Sammy fits into this. Are you saying they all want to marry her and possibly make her another offer at the same time - for money?"

"Pretty much."

"That's disgusting."

"I agree."

"I'm going to tell her so they don't make a fool of her."

"If you do, you run the risk of her doing it to spite you."

"She wouldn't."

I hear my words and know she most definitely would and if I say anything I would also betray Jake's trust in me, which is something I'm happy to have earned.

He watches me with interest and after running every scenario through my mind, I make up my mind.

"Fine." I sigh and throw my hands up in the air. "Have it your way but know that I will be doing everything possible to put her off any crazy scheme they come up with."

"That's fair. Thank you."

"You're welcome."

"No, seriously, Florence, I really appreciate it. My brothers may be idiots most of the time, but their hearts are in the right place. They wouldn't hurt anyone, not knowingly anyway. Maybe Marcus would, actually Brad's a bit of a player when it comes to it. Dom is probably the best bet."

"What do you mean?"

"He's the sort who would fall in love regardless and be happy to play the dutiful husband forever more."

"Then he gets my vote."

Thinking about it, this could work well for both of them because Sammy is in need of some guidance right now and if what Jake says is true and Dom has fallen for her already, this could just be the happy ever after both of them deserve.

Grinning at Jake, I say firmly, "Then team Dom, it is."

"Thanks Florence."

He looks at me as if I am his one true love, and it makes me stop for a moment just to stare. In fact, I could stare into his eyes all night long because Jake is like every romantic hero I've ever imagined, all rolled up into one delicious man.

Part of me is disappointed that he isn't playing the same game because after all, I do have a wedding dress unused and ready to go at a moment's notice and it would be the perfect revenge running off into the sunset with a man like him.

I wonder if he'll change his mind before the cruise returns home. Maybe I should try at least and we could have a joint wedding.

25

We dock in the British Virgin Islands before we even wake up and just seeing dry land through the blind is enough to have me reaching for my clothes in a nanosecond.

"We're here Sammy Jo, hurry up."

She wakes up and rubs her eyes and blinks against the sunshine.

"What time is it?"

"Adventure time."

We share a grin because there is nothing we like more than an adventure and it has certainly come at the right time because last night was heavy in a lot of ways.

When Sammy Jo returned from her meeting with Marcus, she appeared a little distracted – worried even, which made me wonder if he had just come right out with it and asked her to marry him on the spot. Then again, she wouldn't have been able to keep that bottled up and so I'm wondering what the conversation involved.

We don't waste long at breakfast and bump into Ellen and Geoffrey on our way off the ship.

"Darlings, are you heading to shore; such a lovely day for it?"

"Yes, and yes." I smile and Ellen looks between us.

"So, any update on love, you must be halfway through the programme already. Are there any front runners you need a second opinion on?"

Just thinking of the stupid programme makes me wonder whether to pull out and Sammy nods thoughtfully. "You know, Ellen, I am loving every minute of it and it's certainly thrown up a few surprises. I'm undecided yet but there's still time before I have to make a decision."

"And you, Florence, is there anyone special on your horizon?"

Sammy looks a little anxious, and it feels as if she is staring into my soul as I say awkwardly, "Oh, nobody special – I think."

"You think, you mean there may be a potential suitor?"

"Perhaps, oh I don't know, I still think it's too early for me to think about another man in my life."

"Nonsense, there's always room for another one, isn't that right, Geoffrey?"

Ellen giggles as Geoffrey nods and grabs her hand. "Leave the poor girls alone. They will find their own way without you interfering. Honestly, Ellen, you're never satisfied."

They share a loaded look that stuns me a little and as they head off, Sammy whispers, "I told you."

"What?"

"Ellen and Geoffrey are constantly at it by my reckoning."

"Do you think?" If anything, I feel quite jealous of Ellen. Not for being with Geoffrey, of course, but for being settled. Third time lucky it seems. Maybe that will be me in the future. Finally finding my soul mate after many years of trying.

"Do you think that will ever be us?"

"Do you want it to be?"

Sammy seems a little subdued and I wonder what's happened because my friend is never down and is nothing but enthusiastic at all times.

"Yes, I think I do. Isn't that what makes life worthwhile? Finding someone to share it with. Your soul mate, the man who completes your world and makes everything count."

"What if you never find him, what then, do you settle for second best?"

I wonder if she's thinking about her unrequited love. Mind you, it could be a number of men. The list is growing by the day.

"I think he's out there and fate plays a hand in sending him our way. We may make mistakes along the way - Oliver as a prime example, but something changed to steer us on the right path and everything happens for a very good reason, at least that's what I think, anyway."

"Yes, you're probably right."

We reach the exit and as the brilliant sun hits us, I reach for my shades. Bring on another day in paradise. I am so ready for this.

∽

Maybe it's in the name, but I feel so at home on the British Virgin Islands. We take a short taxi ride to downtown St Thomas and enjoy a shopping experience like no other.

The fact it all appears to be duty free is a major plus point and we have soon acquired a couple of handbags and some jewellery that certainly lifts our already high spirits.

Grabbing a cool drink on the edge of the sea, we look out over paradise, and Sammy sighs.

"This is so beautiful. I'm still pinching myself that I'm here at all."

"Me too. I'm glad I'm spending time with you Sammy; I just want to thank you."

"For what?"

"For coming with me. I don't think I would be having half as much fun without you here and as for the cruising in love programme, well, that would have passed me by entirely."

"Would you have still come if I couldn't make it?"

She looks thoughtful, and I nod. "Probably, but it would be less appealing on my own. I suppose my mum could have come with me, or my parents could have enjoyed it instead leaving me to deal with the repercussions of the wedding. I wonder what will be waiting for us when we get home?"

"Unemployment." Sammy sighs and raises her glass to mine. "To life, opportunities and making the most of them whatever they may be."

As we clink glasses, I wonder what that will mean for her because if Jake is right, she will soon have a very important decision to make.

～

WE SPEND a lovely day on shore and as we leave it behind, I wonder if I'll ever be back. I certainly hope so because this place is truly beautiful. A tropical paradise where life takes a moment to reflect and regenerate. I know this island was devastated in a recent hurricane but you would never know it. Somehow, against all the odds, it pieced itself together again and emerged even more beautiful. I am sure it bears the scars of a turbulent time and for some, life will never be the same again.

As I sip my wine and lean over the balcony, I think about my own battle scars that could have destroyed me. Like this island, will I recover? Will I look back and learn from an event that was out of my control? Some storms you never see coming and when they hit, they catch you out. Some you can plan for and weather them as best you can. It's the unknown ones that do the most damage and something tells me that I'm fast approaching another one.

"What are you thinking?"

Sammy steps beside me and takes up a similar pose on the rail and as we stand side by side, looking out across paradise, it strikes me we are both at a junction, unsure of which way to turn.

"I was thinking about the future and wondering what it will bring."

"A life spent doing things like this – hopefully."

She sounds a little wistful and I say gently, "Do you want to talk about it?"

"About what?"

"Whatever's troubling you."

"Who says anything is?"

"You don't need to tell me, it's in your eyes."

"Then I'll wear shades." She sighs and turns with her back to the rail and seems a little troubled.

"What about you, Florrie, how are you feeling? I know you've been through a lot lately and I suppose I've been so busy trying to make you forget, I've forgotten that."

"I'm fine. To be honest, I'm feeling a little guilty that I'm not more upset. That tells me what happened was the right thing. It's the future that scares me, but it's exciting, don't you think?"

"Yes." She seems quiet and I wonder if it has something to do with last night, so I say with interest, "What happened at your meeting, you never did tell me?"

"Well…" She looks a little worried, and my heart sinks. Is this the part that I tell her everything, even though I promised I wouldn't? As soon as Jake told me it was a secret and not to tell anyone, I would have promised him anything just to hear it. I've always been like that, curious and now I know what they have planned and my friend is centre stage in the starring role. To be honest, it sounded like a scene from Seven Brides for Seven Brothers and knowing Sammy Jo, she would be happy with any of them or *all* of them. I wouldn't even put that past her.

Now I know the big secret, I'm not sure if I'm strong enough to keep it and fully expect I'll hear myself telling her *'don't tell anyone you know, but…'* in a matter of seconds.

She sounds nervous as she says, "Marcus, well, he um, offered me the job if I want it."

"Really." My voice sounds unnaturally high, and I wonder what particular job he offered her. Come to think of it, it's probably the wife one because she can't appear to look me in the eye and has been subdued all day. She knows I'll disapprove and try to talk her out of it, then we will fight and probably fall out, which isn't a good idea when you're sleeping with the enemy in a stateroom that is certainly not the size of a small state.

"He wants me to work in his estate agency. You know, the job he described and I'm tempted."

For some reason I feel a surge of relief and smile brightly. "Well, that's good, isn't it? You can work remotely and still get to enjoy nights out with yours truly in search of our happily ever after."

Now she looks extremely uncomfortable and my intuition tells me this job offer is not as straight forward as I think.

"It may not be as easy as that, Florence."

"What do you mean?"

I hold my breath as she sighs and turns around to look at the disappearing shore line.

"I will need to relocate because he wants me to work with him, not for him. It will mean I'm moving almost as soon as we return because he hasn't any time to waste."

"You're moving, but how?"

"He told me an apartment comes with the job. It would start as soon as I could get there. The thing is…"

"What?" My anxiety is at an all-time high as I wait for the punchline and she looks at me through troubled eyes.

"I don't want to hurt you, Florence, you've been through so much already."

"Why would you working for Marcus hurt me?"

"Because you like him and may be annoyed that I'm taking a job you wanted?"

"Do you really think that?" I'm a little stunned because I'm not sure if I would relocate, anyway.

"It wouldn't change anything though." She starts to speak quickly. "It's just that if you like him, I'm not in the way of that, it's just, well, it's just a job."

"Yes, it's just a job, no problem."

It feels a little awkward because I'm not sure if she's being completely honest with me and how can I ask her if she's agreed to another kind of job?

The ship moves effortlessly through the Caribbean water and Sammy says slightly guiltily, "He's asked if I'll meet him later to discuss the arrangements."

"Oh."

"Yes, um, at dinner. Of course, I won't leave you to dine

alone. I'll have dinner with you first and then maybe something small with him, it's just…"

"Just what?"

"I really want this, Florence." She sighs heavily. "This is the first opportunity that's ever come my way that I'm excited about. I know I've always been good academically, but there was never anything I wanted to do that required good grades. Working at the factory was great because I got to have fun and leave work behind at five o'clock every day. There were endless parties and social gatherings, and I loved working there. Then it got boring really quickly and I never really knew what I'd do next. Then you had your heart broken, and I saw a ray of hope attached with my name on it."

"I'm glad I could help." I laugh softly because if my heart is broken, I'm not in the middle of the ocean right now and I say brightly, "You do whatever is right for you, Sammy Jo. If anyone deserves it, you do. This is an amazing opportunity that has your name stamped all over it and who knows, it may take you places you never dreamed of?"

"Funny you should say that."

"What?"

"Dreamed of because that's just where I'm heading."

She laughs and a little of her shine is restored as she smiles. "The apartment is situated in Dream Valley. How cool is that?"

"You're kidding."

"I'm not. Marcus told me it's a town a little way from the sea on the south coast. Dream Valley is a small town with big ideas and that's why he needs me there. It's expanding and will soon be home to a whole new community and he is planning on being the one in control of that. He needs an assistant, somebody to work with him, which is why he asked me. So, you see, Florence, this certainly is the opportunity of a lifetime and I would be a fool to pass it by."

She looks at her phone and raises her eyes. "Goodness, we should go. I have to meet him in ninety minutes and we haven't eaten. We are also due to our next meet and greet with two more dates in thirty minutes. It's all go at sea, isn't it?"

As we head off, I'm glad to see she's back to her usual bright self, but there's still the part of me that worries where this whole thing is heading. Then there's Marcus. When I first met him, I was immediately besotted. There was something so compelling about him and I thought he felt a connection with me too. Then Jake came along and messed with my mind, and Marcus turned his attention to my friend. Is this what they do, play women off against one another? I kind of think that could be the case because these brothers are trouble and if I'm sure of anything, it's that.

26

Tonight's date isn't so bad. Gregory Chambers is an architect who never got around to dating – his actual words – and has now discovered he needs to pull out all the stops if he wants his dream family by the time he's forty.

He's a little serious but not unpleasant and is probably the most normal date I've had so far.

"So, Florence, tell me about your school life. What qualifications did you obtain?"

"That's a bit of a sore subject, Gregory, or can I call you Greg?"

"Gregory's fine."

"Oh, well, um, I never really did well at school and left with the minimum."

"I see."

For some reason it feels as if he's interviewing me for the job as his significant other and it amuses me a little to see the concentration on his face.

"Ok, then tell me what happened after school."

"Oh, that's easy, I started my own business."

"Interesting, tell me more."

He leans forward and a waft of his aftershave hits me and I lean back because it's a little overpowering.

"I started Beauty to Go when I finished my college course. I was always interested in beauty and art and the two go hand in hand. So, I offer a mobile service, you know, go to people's homes when they have a function to attend. Weddings, birthdays, anything really."

"It sounds as if you are quite successful. I like that in a woman."

I bask a little in the admiration in his eyes because it's not often I get complimented on my business sense. Oliver always thought I played at it and never took it seriously. He used to change the subject if I ever spoke about it and wave his hands as if batting away the subject as uninteresting. Gregory is interested and I suppose I must bore him a little when I spend the next thirty minutes telling him all the gossip from the various events I have been asked to cater for and it's only when he looks at his watch, do I feel a little bad.

"So, Gregory, are you here on this cruise alone?"

"No, I'm here with my mother."

"Really, that's…"

"Sad."

"I never said that."

"I expect you thought it though." He sighs and leans forward, whispering, "Don't look now but the woman in green by the bar is my mother. She insisted on coming to all my dates to evaluate the applicants."

Now I really want to turn and see her and it's almost impossible to remain staring at him with a look of abject horror.

"What does she think so far, are there any serious contenders?"

Gregory nods. "She likes Jenny Abbott from Cornwall. Said she was an ordinary looking girl who would fit in with our family rather well. In fact, I believe they have enjoyed afternoon tea together while I was attending the chess competition. Mother said that Jenny would make a personable wife and an excellent mother. I'm afraid it looks as if the jury has already reached its verdict."

He looks at me with such a smug expression I don't have words because if he even thinks he was in the running for any kind of second date with me, he was mistaken. In fact, this whole debacle is making me wish I'd never signed up for this whole nightmare and so I just smile. "I'm happy for you. I'm guessing Jenny is the one then. What if she doesn't choose you though, that could be a problem?"

"Then I will mark you as second choice."

"Gosh thanks."

I meant it to come out as sarcastic, but he obviously didn't hear that and leans back with a smug expression on his face. "Yes, this is shaping up to be a very good idea. An easy way to deal with the intricacies of dating with guaranteed results at the end. I don't know why everyone doesn't choose a partner this way, it's so satisfying."

My blood starts to boil and I snap, "Don't be so sure Gregory, I mean, it's all roses now, but they have thorns, as I know only too well. You may find Jenny has other ideas and my number one may steal your second choice."

"So, you have a number one, then. Who is he?"

"You know Gregory, never mind."

He looks confused as I sigh. "To be honest, I need to be somewhere, anyway. Good luck with Jenny, I'm sure you'll be very happy. It was nice meeting you."

He looks surprised as I head off and pass his mother as I leave. Flashing her a blinding smile, I lean down and whisper, "Just in case you were wondering, your son is definitely not my type and I hope for Jenny's sake, she finds someone way more exciting to spend the last week with. Have a nice evening."

Her look of horror makes me smile as I leave the bar and just the thought of another three dates is making me wish I had never agreed to this.

As I make my way to my room, I feel a little lost at sea. Sammy is probably already on her date with Marcus, and part of me is worried about that. I'm sure he has more than the job on his mind and I'm wishing I had told her - prepared her at least so she could make an informed decision and not fall into his trap.

As I press the button for the elevator, all I want is an early night, but as I step inside, I am quickly joined by a man who appears to be shadowing my every move.

"Jake."

"Hey, surely you're not heading off to bed already."

"To be honest, I was. It's been a long day and well, I'm not that great with my own company and Sammy is with your brother Marcus. What's all that about, by the way, he's offered her a job and she's accepted?"

"I know."

To my surprise, he takes my hand and says firmly, "Come with me."

"Where?"

"Anywhere but bed." He stops and something about the look in his eyes makes my heart flutter as he leans in and whispers, "Let me take you on a date, Florence. Just the two of us with no stupid competition, no ulterior motive, just a man who finds a woman insanely attractive and will do anything to make her look at him in the same way."

For a moment I just stare at him in complete surprise

and he looks so uncertain standing there, looking at me with his puppy dog eyes, I forget everything in this moment but the fact I am already insanely attracted to him.

My voice sounds weak as I whisper, "Ok."

His smile is breath taking as his fingers lace with mine and he says huskily, "Step on board Cinderella, our coach has arrived."

He pulls me after him, and I wonder what he has in mind. Why he has it in mind and what state my heart will be at the end of the night?

27

Our first stop was the aqua show, which was so much fun. It felt good sitting beside a man like Jake, who definitely knows how to have a good time. We followed that with a comedy show which brightened my mood and now we are sitting in deck chairs on the promenade deck, eating ice creams and gazing at the stars.

"Are you happy, Florence?"

Jake's question takes me by surprise, and I take a minute before answering him.

"I think so."

"Only think?" He sounds a little hurt, and I nod. "I shouldn't be. If I had any kind of heart, it should be broken right now but it's as if I've left the old me behind and discovered a much more exciting version at sea."

"I like the new version. In fact, I probably would have liked the old version too."

He smiles, and as his leg brushes against mine, I feel a shiver of desire. It hasn't escaped my notice that I am currently on a date with the hottest guy I have ever seen and he appears to like me, too. That worries me a little because what if he's just passing time and will head off home when this ship anchors and become a luxurious memory? I decide to do a little digging and discover more about this perfect stranger.

"So, tell me more about your father's plans for you all. How are your brother's coping; have they found anyone suitable yet?"

I swirl my tongue around the delicious creamy delight in a cone and Jake watches me with a lust-filled look, making the air between us super-charged and exciting.

He leans back, and the spell is broken as he says casually, "Dom is still set on Sammy Jo even though he had a good date with Clarissa."

"Tell me about her."

"She's ok, quite nice actually but I think he's onto a loser there."

"Why?"

"Because I dated her the night before and she invited me back to her stateroom for a test drive."

My mouth hovers on the cone as I register only one word, *date*. Jake is still dating available women.

He laughs and whispers, "I say date. It was another one of these set ups and I'm only going along because I have nothing better to do. For some reason my heart isn't in it anymore."

"Why not?"

"It never was to be honest, then I met a girl who ticked every box I ever had and added a few more."

"I see."

My world comes crashing down because Jake must have met someone already and I look up in surprise as he says, "Look at me, Florence."

I do as he says and the look in his eyes makes me hold

my breath as he whispers, "You. I met you. By mistake admittedly, but I knew as soon as I saw you struggling on your date with the eco vegan. There was something about you that interested me which is why I rescued you from eternal dullnation."

"Don't you mean damnation?"

"No, dullnation because a woman like you needs excitement, adventure and the fairy-tale."

"How do you know?"

To be honest, he can keep talking all night if he wants to because I like every word that falls from his lips. Then he reaches forward and plucks the cone from my hand, laying it gently on a discarded plate on the table beside us. I watch in anticipation as he leans forward until his lips are almost touching mine and says huskily, "I want you, Florence. No other woman, just you."

His mouth is so close I could shift and land on it with zero effort at all, but something makes me hold back because I'm not sure if this is all an act and he has an ulterior motive.

As his eyes gleam in the darkness, there's the reckless part of me that will worry about that later, because the most important thing right now is to indulge the fantasy. So what if this lasts as long as the cruise, at least I would have fun and a memory to treasure? Picturing Oliver snuggling up to his wife and thinking of Sammy Jo and her tale of the one who got away, I owe it to myself to run with this and so as his lips touch mine, I let the moment take me with it because kissing Jake in the moonlight, is sweeter than any ice cream with chocolate sauce and all the works and I owe it to my future self to create a memory I will treasure forever.

We kiss under the stars, then we kiss on the dance floor at the seventies disco to *How Deep Is Your Love*.

We share many kisses in the audience of Songs from Broadway and he nibbles my neck as we wait with bated breath at the million-dollar lottery draw in the Casino Royale. By the time we stop kissing, it's because we have reached the lower deck and are heading towards my stateroom, and now it feels a little awkward.

Do I invite him in? I would be breaking my own rule of course, and Sammy Jo may already be there, anyway. Should I offer him a night cap on the balcony and slip into something comfortable and ask him to paint me like Jack does Rose on the Titanic?

A door slamming makes me stop agonising over where we go from here, and as I look up, I stare in horror at the trio emerging from a room just down the hall from mine.

"Oh my god."

"What is it, do you know those people?"

"Florence, darling."

Ellen and Geoffrey bear down on us, and I look at the third person with horror. Norman.

"Look who we found; it's a small world isn't it, darling?"

Ellen pulls Norman forward, who appears to have his shirt on inside out. Come to think of it, Ellen looks a little flushed and Geoffrey is beaming as if he's won that jackpot lottery.

"Who is this delightful man with you?"

"Oh, um, this is Jake."

"Hudson, I'm pleased to meet you." Jake steps forward and shakes all of their hands and Ellen beams with obvious approval.

"Well, darling, my advice certainly paid off, he's gorgeous."

Ellen flashes Jake a rather disturbing look and then

pulls Norman forward. "I believe you've had the pleasure of Norman already."

I squirm a little as he says, "Yes, we've dated. How are things going Florence?"

Jake is struggling to stop laughing as I say tightly, "Fine, thank you. How about you, are you still looking?"

Ellen grins and I feel a little disturbed by the look she gives him and then leans forward and whispers, "Don't tell anyone, but we've been enjoying illicit adventures in Norman's cabin. I told you a cruise can be so much fun if you open your mind and leave your principles behind you."

I daren't look at anyone actually because I feel a little sea sick right now and Ellen says, "Cards, darling. Strip poker mainly, but there is always the incentive of a few dollars to spice up the action. Geoffrey is a master at it and Norman enjoys the odd hand of an evening, so we get one in before bedtime. You should join us tomorrow night."

"No." It comes out way louder than I intended and I say with a deep breath, "Thank you. I'm not very good at cards and would probably lose."

"Then I insist you join us."

Norman leers at me very inappropriately and Jake steps in and says firmly, "I'm sorry, but I have other plans for Florence. It was nice meeting you but we should really be going."

He pulls me off, and I feel mortified when I see the knowing looks on their faces and I hiss, "What did you say that for, now they'll think we're…"

"What?"

"You know."

"No, I don't."

He is struggling to keep the laughter from his eyes and I

feel a little heated when I think about what that would involve, and he laughs softly and pulls me to a stop.

"Relax, babe. My intentions are strictly honourable. My plan is to see you to your cabin and kiss you goodnight. Isn't that what a gentleman would do?"

"Oh, of course."

We reach my cabin and Jake pulls me into his arms, that are becoming quite familiar by now, and lowers his lips to mine and whispers, "I'll see you at breakfast. Spend the day with me."

"I can't." I groan "I've got some kind of crazy breakfast date lined up. Cruise ship Bobby would be really annoyed if I didn't show up."

"Then after, we could spend the day in St Maarten together."

"Ok." I smile happily because that sounds like a dream come true. Then I think of Sammy and groan. "I should go with Sammy; I can't leave her."

"I'll sort something out, leave it with me."

Jake kisses me as if he's desperate for air. It's so intense, so sexy, and messes with my mind. I am trying so hard to be good. To hold back and play it cool, but he makes it impossible to.

Jake Hudson is extremely bad for my health and I'm in danger of catching a bad dose of heartache as a result.

28

Sammy Jo doesn't roll in until past 3am and I only know that because as she gets into bed, she curses as she knocks something on to the floor.

I pretend to be asleep but note the time on the clock by my bed. Now I'm awake I can't sleep and her even breathing tells me she doesn't have the same trouble.

Now I've met Jake, I'm no longer interested in Marcus. We certainly never clicked as much as I do with Jake and yet there's something troubling me about the whole thing. I still have a feeling they are playing a bigger game and I'm not certain of anything anymore.

~

THE MORNING BRINGS with it a day full of action and I think carefully about what I wear. Sammy Jo emerges from the shower and sits on the edge of the bed, combing out her wet hair and looks a little worried which isn't like her.

"Are you ok?"

"Yes, are you?"

"Me." She nods. "Of course, why wouldn't I be?"

She appears to be weighing up her words carefully. "May I ask you a personal question, Florrie?"

"Of course."

"Do you like Marcus?"

"In what way?"

"Any way."

She looks troubled and I wonder if she means romantically or as a person, so I shrug. "When I first met him, I thought he was good looking and there was something that attracted me to him. However, now I've met Jake I'm not as interested in Marcus, unless of course he still has a job for me. That does sound like fun."

I smile and she nods thoughtfully. "I think he does. He asked me if you were still interested, are you?"

"Of course, but I'm not sure I'd be interested enough to move home for it."

"I don't think you'd have to. He needs people all around the country who could head over and do the viewings at a moment's notice. It's quite a set up he's got there."

"So, you had a good evening then."

I'm not sure if it's my imagination or not but she looks a little troubled and the warning sirens sound inside my head. "The thing is, Florence I'm worried."

I knew it. I lean forward with interest. "Go on."

"I'm just worried that you like him and I've interfered with that. The last thing I wanted to do was upset you in any way."

"You haven't."

Sitting beside her, I smile encouragingly. "I might have liked him a little at the start but nothing more. I quite like his brother though."

"You know they're brothers?"

She seems a little surprised by that and I wonder what he's told her.

"Of course. I know there are four of them and they are here because their dad died."

"And…" She listens earnestly and I feel a little uncomfortable because now is obviously the time to come clean.

"I know they all like you and are in some kind of competition to win the final week with you."

"So I believe."

"He told you."

"Yes." She nods. "He told me Dom and Brad were having some kind of war over who gets to date me in the final week. It's a little sad really; I don't want to come between brothers."

"And Marcus, where does he fit into all this?" I hold my breath as I wait for her to tell me everything and she shrugs. "He doesn't. He's just my new boss I suppose. He did tell me that Jake likes you but is worried."

"About what?"

"That you're vulnerable. You may not be ready to meet someone and he's holding back a little because of it."

I'm stunned because if Jake's holding back, I wonder what he's like when he's operating at full speed. The thought makes me feel dizzy and I shrug. "Maybe but I'm not thinking about the past. Just the future counts now and as you said, I need to be open to opportunity. You see, Sammy, you have taught me a valuable lesson and that's to live for the day. Oliver is so far behind me I sometimes forget he was meant to be here. It's what happens next that counts and if you're saying Jake is holding back, then I'll make it obvious he needn't bother."

"But what if you're just rebounding? You could be."

"Have you seen him? Honestly, Sammy, that man makes

Oliver look like an amateur. My only concern is that he's using me because he's bored. I can't seem to shake that feeling but have decided to run with it anyway. I'm like a younger Shirley Valentine feeling her way through life. I'll either run off into the sunset with the sexy stranger, or return to normality. Whichever way, I'll have had fun doing it, so don't be concerned for me, just concentrate on your own happiness, it's all I want."

"You're a good friend, Florrie."

"Right back at you, babe."

We share a watery smile and as the ship's horn sounds, we both jump and Sammy grins. "Then dates for breakfast it is."

She hesitates a little and then says awkwardly, "I hope you don't mind but Marcus asked if I would spend the day with him at St Maartens. Probably just to go over a few things at lunch. Do you mind, I know we had plans to go together?"

"No, that's fine. Jake kind of mentioned going together anyway but I said I'd see what you were doing first."

She looks relieved which makes me feel better and as she turns to finish getting ready, I am looking forward to the day ahead with a little less guilt attached.

29

The man opposite me at breakfast is one I never thought I'd see. Dom, Jake's brother is looking at me with interest and I'm feeling a little intimidated if I'm honest. First Marcus, then Jake, and now Dom's attention is blinding me. He is every bit as gorgeous as his brothers, but in a darker way. Marcus is guarded and certainly doesn't wear his emotions in full view. Jake is easier to get along with, funny and considerate, not to mention sexy and so good looking he could be a model or actor.

Dom, however, is more serious, brooding and is looking at me in a way that makes me blush a little and imagine all sorts of dirty thoughts. Slight stubble grazes his chin and his dark flashing eyes promise more excitement than a girl could stand. A serious Christian Grey contender and I squirm a little on my seat as he fills my glass with water and says in a deep voice, "I was curious."

"In what way?"

"To meet the girl who has turned my brother's head."

"Which one." I make light of it, and he smiles briefly. "Jake. Unless there's something I don't know about."

"No, I only know your other brother Marcus and he's offered me a job, so things are going well, I think."

"Will you take it – the job I mean?"

"Maybe, although he's offered my friend a different kind of job."

I phrase it that way to test his reaction and he raises his eyes and looks a little put out.

"I heard."

"Jake told me you like her."

"I do."

I am coming to the conclusion that Dom is a man of very few words, and the only ones he speaks are the ones he needs to. There is no polite chit chat, just a way to get to the point in the least time possible.

I clear my throat. "So, Jake told me of your challenge. I must say I was a little worried, shocked even."

"In what way?"

"In every way." I lower my voice. "You are pursuing my friend as some kind of mail-order bride, not to mention potential mother to your children. I think I have the right to be concerned as well as deeply shocked by the whole situation."

"Have you told her?" He looks a little worried and I pause before sighing and saying tersely, "No, but I'm seriously thinking of it. I don't want her to be used, she deserves more."

"I see."

He looks thoughtful, and I'm wondering if I'll ever get the truth from these guys. I have a feeling there's a bigger picture I'm missing somewhere, and it's on a strictly need to know basis.

After a short, tense silence, Dom says, "I like your friend, a lot and if anyone's worried about her situation, it's me."

"Why, what's happened?"

"Marcus is interfering in something for his own personal gain and, for some reason, is intent on destroying my own plans. Now part of me wonders if it's because of his own selfish desires, or something else."

"He's your brother, ask him."

"We may be brothers." He shakes his head sadly. "But we have different agendas. None of us do anything with family loyalty in mind. I expressed an interest in Sammy Jo and suddenly all my brothers are interested, except for Jake, of course."

He smiles and I stare at him in surprise because it looks wrong on him. It transforms his face and suddenly shows me a different side to him. A better side and as fast as it appeared, he shuts down again and sighs.

"Listen. Out of all my brothers, Sammy Jo would be better off with me. I'm loyal, would treat her right and interested in her as a person, not for what she can give me."

The words taste bitter as I say harshly, "I expect you're talking about your inheritance."

"So, he did tell you." He leans back in his seat and shakes his head. "Why am I not surprised?"

"It's ok, I haven't told her yet but I will if I think you're using her."

He sighs and leans forward. "My father was a conniving tyrant. He wanted control and when he lost it, he thought of a devious plan to control us from the grave. We have agonised over this and thought of every way out of it but the best thing for everyone involved is to see it through."

"You would say that."

"Yes, I would, and I will keep on saying it. Jake doesn't care about it because he gets what he wants, regardless."

"What do you mean?"

Dom's eyes flash and he laughs softly. "So, he didn't tell you everything then."

"Tell me what?"

Suddenly, I really need to know this and he shrugs. "It's not for me to say. The only thing I need you to know is that Sammy is better off with me. Marcus is interfering in something out of greed, and not for the right reasons. I need to marry first, for everyone's sakes. So please, Florence, help me persuade Sammy Jo to stick with me and I promise she will be more than happy with the outcome. I'm attracted to her, I enjoy her company and I want to see where this will lead and I would even without this stupid inheritance making my decisions for me, so please, will you help me?"

He looks so serious and so believable and thinking about Marcus, he does seem the nicer option. As I pour us both another coffee from the pot, I say with a sigh, "It's not up to me, Dom. It is and always will be Sammy's choice. Just so you know, if she asks, I will tell her everything I know. Until she asks, I'll keep it to myself and let her heart decide because the most important thing in all of this is that Sammy Jo is happy."

"What about you?"

"Me?"

"Don't you want to be happy?"

"Of course."

"Do you think Jake can make you happy because if you do, you need to know something about him."

Now all of my nerve endings are standing to attention desperate to hear every reason why I should run and hide and Dom says gruffly, "Jake is not the marrying kind, not the settling down type and if it's that kind of future you're after, you won't find it with him."

"Why not?" I really need to know this, and Dom shrugs. "He's happy just the way he is – alone."

"But why? Surely everyone wants to meet someone special and settle down."

"He already has."

His words crush my soul, and he laughs softly. "Jake only needs one person in his life and he looks at him every time he stares into the mirror. Jake is selfish, unconcerned with responsibility and a free spirit who would mess up any relationship inside of a year. I'm just warning you of that because as a friend of Sammy's, I want you to be happy. Remember, I would make her happy and this is my gift to you, to show you I mean business even at the expense of my brother's wishes."

Wow, this family is something else. They make Machiavellian their middle name. I don't think any of them are playing for the team right now and so I just nod and smile gratefully. "Thanks for telling me, I'll bear it in mind."

We finish up, and before we leave the table, Jake heads our way and smiles. "Hey, mind if I interrupt your date and whisk the fair lady to paradise?"

Dom rolls his eyes. "As if you care what I think."

"You know me so well, brother."

Dom stands and smiles politely. "It was a pleasure to meet you, Florence. Remember what I said."

He grins at his brother and I see a little smirk of triumph ghost his lips as Jake looks annoyed.

As soon as he leaves, Jake reaches for my hand and rolls his eyes. "Whatever my brother told you, take it with a pinch of salt because that man is playing a dangerous game and we are the poor sods caught up in the crossfire."

As we walk away, I'm left feeling even more confused than before. What is going on and why do I feel like I'm balancing on a cliff edge and am about to fall?

30

Walking with Jake is certainly a pleasurable experience and reminds me that I should have had a man by my side this entire time. It feels a little different somehow, and although Sammy is great company, there is something more intimate about having a man beside me.

I love the way he holds my hand and helps me from the boat. The way he immediately takes charge of the itinerary after having asked me what I would like to do first. It feels good being fussed over, and I can't remember the last time I was. Oliver was always too busy with work to organise fun days out. If we did anything it was because I had arranged it and he was never one for surprises and everything was always methodically planned – by me.

Now I'm seeing what it's like when a man takes charge and even though the feminist inside me is roaring at this, the woman in me is lapping up the attention and content to let him get on with it.

"This is so pretty."

We walk down the little rows of houses in Phillipsburg,

St Maarten's and Jake nods. "Yes, the island is part Dutch, part French and you can definitely see the Dutch influence here."

I look in awe at the pastel-coloured houses with second story verandas and courtyards filled with the most beautiful flowers.

"Did you know this is also known as the land of salt?" He says casually, and I shake my head. "Goodness, no I didn't."

"Yes, in the seventeenth century, the Dutch settlers harvested it from the salt pond and sent it back to Europe. Can you imagine how many days that would have taken? We take for granted our ability to do things in a much easier way."

"It must have been very different back then."

I smile and look around, falling in love with such a beautiful place almost immediately, which is about right for me. I'm always impressionable and easily pleased, which is why I probably agreed to marry Oliver in the first place.

"Would you like to visit the Butterfly Farm, I heard it's an experience not to be missed?" His suggestion surprises me but it does sound like fun so I nod, "I would love to."

We decide to grab a taxi, but as soon as we tell him where we want to go, he shakes his head.

"I'm sorry, it's closed."

I feel a little disappointed about that because it is something I've never done before and was looking forward to expanding my knowledge a little.

"The hurricane forced it to close. Maybe you can take the Rhino Rider speed boat instead."

"The what?"

Jake grins, but I look down at my strappy sandals and wonder if this is such a good idea.

"Hey, that sounds fun, I'm game if you are."

He looks so excited I don't have the heart to disappoint him, and so I nod. "Ok, let's give it a go."

Before long we find ourselves at Cole Bay, being given a safety talk as we wear lifejackets and join several other excited couples looking for adventure.

Now I'm here, I'm quite looking forward to the next two hours because I get to spend the entire time holding tightly onto Jake. We are soon in our little yellow boat and as my arms reach around his broad upper torso, I feel as if all my Christmases have come at once and I congratulate myself on a good choice.

We are soon on the water and follow our guide along with our fellow adventure seekers, on the way to the appropriately named Happy Bay.

It feels good to be on the water and just speeding along, feeling the wind in my hair and the salt on my skin, makes me feel so alive. This is what life is all about. Experiencing different things. Enjoying the sunshine and making every second count and just imagining my usual day, seems like a different world away. Now I understand why people travel and just take off and see where the world takes them. You get to visit beautiful places that are so different from the ones you usually see on a daily basis. Picturing the slightly grey skies of home and the drizzling rain seems almost unbelievable when faced with wall to wall sunshine and beautiful turquoise seas.

By the time we reach Happy Bay I am glad we came and when we pull up on the shore, the fact Jake sweeps me into his arms and carries me to the golden sand makes me the happiest woman alive.

Then all my dreams come true as he whips off his t-shirt, revealing the most amazing toned body with abs that dance before my eyes, and I could happily lie back and study it all day.

Luckily, I wore my bikini under my sun dress and before long I join him and as we lie on the powdery white sand gazing up at the sunshine, I have to pinch myself that this is happening at all.

"This is what it's all about, isn't it, Florrie?" Jake sighs with contentment and I have to agree with him.

"It certainly is. Thanks for persuading me. This is a treat I wouldn't have missed for the world."

Jake turns and props himself on his side and looks at me thoughtfully. "Do you travel much?"

"No, once a year to Spain mainly, on a package holiday. This has really opened my eyes."

"So, what happens when you return home?"

Just thinking about my old life against this exciting one fills me with sadness. It doesn't seem that appealing to return to a life of work, rest and work again.

"I suppose I go back to work and see where life takes me."

"So, you don't have any real responsibilities back home then, you mentioned your business is mobile."

"Where is this going, Jake?" I look at him with surprise because he is suddenly looking at me with a serious look in his eyes and I sense change coming.

"Maybe you could come back with me to Dream Valley and we could see where life takes us from there."

I think I'm in shock and just stare at him in utter amazement, not really knowing what to say.

He grins. "We could plan our next adventure, maybe skiing in the alps, or trekking in the jungle somewhere. We should go, it would be fun."

It strikes me that Jake is only out for one thing – fun, which is fine when you're settled and money is no object, but I am far from settled and need to get my life back in order.

"It sounds good, but I have to face facts. My life is a mess and I need to tidy it up. I can't just take off with reckless abandon and see where life takes me, it doesn't work like that."

"Your friend is by the sound of it."

"Maybe because she has no other option right now. Sammy Jo has no job and she rents a room in a flat that she will struggle to afford and she has no ties."

"Do you?"

I think for a moment because what are my ties outside of the usual ones?

"Well, obviously my family, mum, dad and dog Tigger."

"Strange name for a dog." He laughs and I push him hard.

"Tigger bounces a lot. It is the perfect name for him."

"What else?"

I know he is making me face up to the fact I have nothing, and I'm not very happy about that, so I shrug. "I have my business and my customers. That has taken a lot of time and effort to build up from scratch. If I left, someone else would take over my turf."

"What are you, some kind of mafia don or something?"

"You'd better believe it, don't mess with me kid."

Did I really just try to sound like Marlon Brando? I am seriously embarrassed right now.

Jake jumps up. "Come on, let's go for a swim. It sure beats the communal pool on the main deck. This is what real swimming is about."

We run hand in hand into the sea and in moments like this I could agree to anything. This place makes everything possible and if Jake whipped a priest out from behind the palm tree, I would be like Pamela Anderson marrying Tommy Lee on a beach in a bikini. This is why holidays can be extremely bad for your health because they pluck you from reality and make everything possible.

As I frolic in a blue lagoon with a hot guy, I could forgive myself any decision I make. This is what life should be about, surely. Then why do most people settle for 9-5 and a mortgage?

We finish off our trip to St Maarten with a gorgeous meal in one of the French restaurants on the French side. It feels so romantic to be sitting holding hands across the table in paradise with a David Beckham lookalike. The food is good, the company is good, and the scenery is good, which is what I'm blaming my rash decision on because when Jake raises my hand and kisses it softly and looks deep into my eyes, I hold my breath as he says earnestly, "I have a question to ask you, Florrie and I hope you won't think I'm crazy."

My heart starts thumping as I see a serious edge to his expression and I wonder if I'm going to regret the most definite 'yes' I will be answering him with. I can refuse him nothing when he is looking as if I'm his dream come true and he kisses my fingers and stares deep into my eyes and whispers, "Promise you'll choose me to spend next week with because I can't bear the thought of you spending it with anyone else."

"Well, I did have some rather successful dates to choose from." I laugh and pretend to be considering my options.

"I mean, you've met Norman. He is definitely a contender. What about Adam, a little odd maybe, but I'm keen to learn more about his vegan diet and how he intends on forming it into a movement. Then there was Richard. He seems decent enough, perfectly grounded and ready to start again. Or there's your brother, Dom, he was interesting."

Jake tightens his hold on my hand and growls, "Anyone but him."

"Why?"

"Because I don't want to watch him seduce you."

The humour is gone and I stare at him in shock because there's a storm in his eyes that I never saw coming.

"Does he make a habit of that – seducing your girlfriends?"

Sighing, Jake leans back in his seat and shakes his head. "No, of course not, but he's intent on only one thing right now and it appears that anything could happen. You see, Florrie, Dom and Marcus are brothers obviously and share many of the same character traits. Brad and me, well, we're easier going, more laid back and content to roll with the punches. They inherited their ways from my father. He was the same, ruthless, driven, and conniving. Our mum is easy going, slightly forgetful and the sweetest person I have ever met. It's your choice obviously but if you were to spend the week with either of them, they would wrap their web around you and eat you alive. Stick with me and you're safe from that and some say I'm quite good company."

He smiles and looks so hopeful I know immediately I couldn't even think of choosing anyone else. It will always be Jake, but the picture he paints of his brothers is not a pleasant one and the person in the middle of it all is my best friend.

31

The Vitality Spa is a place I should have visited on day one.

As I lie beside my friend, we probably fully relax for the first time while skilled technicians work on our sun ravaged skin.

It was Sammy's idea, a facial rejuvenation experience at the spa before dinner, and I was more than happy to oblige after my day on the beach with Jake.

The beautician looks at me with resignation because I completely forgot to take sunscreen with me and am paying the price for that. Sunburn is a kind way of putting the third-degree burns that appear to have ravaged my once perfect skin. I daren't tell her that I'm a beautician by trade because no doubt she would report me to the authorities and get my certificate confiscated - permanently.

We are left to 'think about what we've done' wrapped in heated towels in a darkened room, and as soon as the door closes Sammy whispers, "I don't think I'll ever leave this place. I'm in heaven."

"I know what you mean, just listen to that whale music, I

must download it to my collection."

"And those candles, I wonder what that scent is?"

"If I was trying to guess, I'd probably say it's lavender, jasmine and Brazilian rosewood, with a hint of citrus, perhaps?"

"You're making that up." Sammy laughs softly and I giggle. "I saw a little sign that explained what scents they use. It pays to be alert at all times."

Sammy sighs with pleasure. "So, tell me, how was your date with the gorgeous Jake. You know, I really think you suit one another, he seems a great guy."

Just thinking of Jake makes me smile and I can't keep the smugness from my voice as I whisper back, "He wants me to spend next week with him. What do you think?"

"Um, yes, of course. He's amazing and way better than that loser, Oliver. It was a good thing he humiliated you and ran off with another woman."

Suddenly, it becomes the funniest thing both of us have ever heard and we can't stop laughing. In fact, as I hold my sides, I wonder if I'm having a mental breakdown brought on by the shock of my wedding. Tears run down my face as I laugh uncontrollably and Sammy is the first to get a word past her laughter and wipes her eyes, saying with a gulp, "This feels so good."

"What does?"

"Laughing. I don't know about you but the past week has been a little intense."

I'm surprised because she appeared to be having the best time ever and she says sadly, "I ran into Joseph on the way back from the shore visit. He was obviously returning from the gym, and we were the only ones in the lift. It was a little awkward, and that's putting it mildly."

"Wow, you never said, what happened?"

"I just came right out and asked him if he was on his honeymoon and he gave me a funny look and told me that he was and yet..."

"What?" I look at her in surprise because this is unexpected, and she nods sadly. "He asked me if I had ever wondered what might have happened between us if that night had turned out differently."

"What did you say?"

"The truth. I told him it had often crossed my mind and that I always thought we had unfinished business."

"You were brave. What did he say?"

"That he felt the same." Even in the dim light, I can see the regret in Sammy's eyes and she shrugs.

"It's too late for that, though. It has to remain firmly in the past because, after all, he is on his honeymoon. He told me he met her at work. They have been dating for three years and are very happy. When he asked me about my own life, it reminded me how little I've done with it. A job in a factory and a credit card bill the size of the national debt. What am I doing, Florrie, why am I such a loser?"

"You're no loser, Sammy, look at you. Firstly, Joseph may be happy now but what happens in ten years from now and has the house, the mortgage, the kids and the knowledge that he never really lived. You are doing things in exactly the right order because you are living your best life before you grow up and make a future with a man you have fallen head over heels in love with. You will find him and have many exciting stories to tell your children when you tuck them into bed at night."

"Maybe not all the stories." She laughs softly and I grin. "No, definitely not all the stories, but you get the idea, don't you. Just live life to the max and leave the growing up part for when you're exhausted. Have fun and step outside your comfort zone and if the only regret you have is that you never got to be Joseph whatever his name is girlfriend, then count yourself lucky. I know I am because what sort of life would I have married to Oliver? No, I'm all about the adventure now and so let's make a pact. Enjoy life and see where it takes us. Don't disregard opportunity when it comes calling because it could be destiny in disguise."

"So, it seems as if you've made some decisions of your own, tell me more."

As she throws my words back at me, it strikes me that I have. I'm not ready to settle down and I'm not ready to stop living, so Jake's way of thinking is definitely rubbing off on me and I say thoughtfully, "You know, I've made my decision. I am spending next week with Jake and whatever happens, I'm going to keep an open mind and put any fear behind me. It's time to start living, Sammy Jo. What about you?"

I'm conscious that I've been thinking of my own situation, whereas hers is a lot more uncertain and she says with a strength that surprises me. "I'm going to do what's right for me and it may shock some people but I can't think about that right now."

"Why, what are you planning?"

"I'm going to work for Marcus and take him up on his offer of an apartment and the job and move to Dream Valley."

"Good for you, Sammy."

To be honest, I feel a little relieved because at least it's just a job. No marriage proposal, just a good old-fashioned job offer. Thinking about the two men who appear to be locked in a weird competition, I wonder how this next week will pan out. One thing's for sure, I'm going to keep a close eye on the situation, for her sake.

32

I'm not sure why we thought this was a good idea, but later, just before dinner we are watching an adult football competition. It appears the Hudson brothers are on the same team for once in their lives as they shout instructions and reveal their competitive edge as they battle it out for supremacy.

Sammy Jo sighs beside me. "They are impressive, aren't they?"

I have to admit she's right because the four brothers are 10/10 in the looks department. Their bodies aren't so bad either, and as I take a sip of my wine, I congratulate myself on hitting the jackpot.

"So, what are your plans after dinner?"

"I'm meeting Marcus."

"Again?" I'm a little surprised because surely they covered all the job stuff earlier at lunch, so I decide to do a little digging.

"So, how was your lunch with him, did you fall in love with St Maarten, I know I did?"

"Hmm."

She sips her drink and I see her staring at Marcus thoughtfully, who is barking orders at Jake as they run down the pitch with the ball.

"What are you thinking?"

"Nothing." She smiles brightly. "I suppose I'm a little worried that I'll let him down. I mean you should see the plans he has; they are so impressive and it's no wonder he needs as many staff as he does."

"Then why hasn't he set up that meeting with me yet?" To be honest, I couldn't care less, but I want to see if he's just making excuses to see her again.

"Oh, I forgot to mention, he asked if we were free tomorrow to go through the training. You don't mind, do you, it would really help?"

"Sure, I'd be delighted."

She carries on studying him, despite the fact Dom keeps on looking her way and I feel a little bad for him. Something is going on with my in-demand friend and I'm determined to get to the bottom of it.

By the time the game ends and the Hudson brothers and their team have been thrashed by the junior under fifteens 3-0, we head off to the bar to wait for them to shower and change.

I love this part of the evening. Pre-dinner cocktails before heading off to sample whatever gourmet treats the Aphrodite has lined up for us.

The first man back is Brad and I watch with interest as he drops a light kiss on the top of Sammy Jo's head and says sweetly, "Evening gorgeous." Then he turns to me and smiles.

"We haven't met yet, I'm Brad, the B stands for best brother."

He grins and grabs a seat beside Sammy Jo and reaches for a beer.

"I always enjoy a game of football; it brings out my competitive edge."

"That appears to run in the family." Sammy laughs and says, "Brad was my date this morning for breakfast. So now the only brother I haven't been paired up with is Jake. How weird is that?"

"Maybe you will be tomorrow. We still have two more dates to endure."

Brad laughs. "Then I hope you're one of mine, Florence. Jake can't stop talking about you and I'd love to see him squirm when it's my turn."

For some reason I am hoping it is him because I want to find out what's going on. There's definitely something mysterious about them and I'm still worried that we will get caught up in it.

Dom is next to arrive and I stifle a grin as he stares daggers at Brad's arm laying carelessly along the back of Sammy's chair.

Watching him with her is interesting though. When he smiles, it takes my breath away. It completely transforms the bad boy look he has going on and makes him almost irresistible. Sammy smiles sweetly at him as he drops in the seat opposite her and says, "You played well. Congratulations."

"Thanks, although Brad wasn't much help."

Brad grins. "Keep telling yourself that. I can outplay you any day of the week."

By the time Marcus and Jake join us, we are drawing a few intense looks from the women around us and I feel quite heated just being among them. Four desirable men in their prime, flanking two women who are spinning around in circles unsure of which way to turn.

"So, is anyone up for country line dancing class. I'm keen to give that a go?" Jake grins and Brad nods enthusiastically. "I'm game for that?"

Marcus growls. "Then have fun, because as soon as I've eaten, I'm heading to the casino. I'm feeling lucky tonight."

For some reason he looks at Sammy as he says it and I notice a pink blush stain her cheeks and the warning sirens almost deafen me. What has happened?

Dom doesn't seem to notice and says, "I was hoping to take Sammy to see the movie, A Star Is Born. She mentioned she wanted to see it and they're showing it tonight."

"Hey are they really, I would love to see it?" Sammy looks excited and I watch with interest as Marcus raises his eyes and the look he shoots his brother would make me shrivel up in terror. However, Dom just throws a triumphant one back at him as Sammy says, "You don't mind, do you, Florrie? We could have dinner and then would you mind if I went to watch it? I'm feeling a little tired anyway and the dancing may be a little too much for me tonight."

"Of course, no problem."

As I sip my cocktail, I'm more confused than ever. It appears that something's going on here and Sammy Jo has her own secrets to guard. Why is nothing ever simple and easy and how have I ended up on National Lampoons honeymoon?

33

Jake and Brad are such good company and I have never laughed so much in my life. We tried desperately to learn line dancing along with many other passengers but all we managed to do was cause chaos and end up dancing a hoedown on the bar to claps and cheers from everyone.

Even the staff encouraged us and I blame the many 'drinks of the day' we consumed, which incidentally was a rather delicious blend of a melon infusion of rum, vodka, sweet & sour grenadine that was shaken with a melon liqueur. It was all rather intoxicating and I will pay dearly tomorrow when I try to use the day to sleep off the night before.

Brad is soon bored however and says he's off to find Marcus and curse his bad luck on the roulette wheel, leaving me and Jake to wander arm in arm on the promenade deck, giggling like kids and attracting disapproving looks from other couples looking for a night stroll before turning in.

Jake's arm is slung around my shoulder and as we reach

the end of the walkway, he pulls me in front of him, just like Jack did to Rose on the Titanic and starts singing, My Heart Will Go On.

Surely this is every woman's dream. So I join him and feel content to be in his arms with the wind and spray cooling my heated skin, reviving me a little as we stare at the twinkling stars that laugh down at us.

I'm not sure how it happens, but Jake spins me around, and then looks deep into my eyes and whispers, "Can I kiss you, Florrie?"

I nod as my eyes sparkle with longing because I will finally get my wish.

Jake's kiss is surprisingly gentle and soft, delicious and sweet. He wraps his hand around the back of my head and pulls me in closer and doesn't appear to be in any hurry to get it over with anytime soon.

Kissing Jake is the best kind of promise. One that has been building all week and one I never thought would happen. It's as if we were made to connect in this way. It feels right somehow and not reckless at all. Oliver who, because it's as if this is my first kiss. It somehow means so much and yet we've only just met.

Is this the moment when planets collide because it certainly feels that way? Life will never be the same again now that Jake and Florence have sealed the deal.

Any doubts I have mean nothing in this moment and if he has an ulterior motive for this, I'm happy about that. Tomorrow is another day when my head will take charge again and I can blame this moment of reckless abandon on the alcohol because absolutely nothing is going to interfere with this life changing moment.

Jake pulls back first and strokes my face lightly, causing a delicious shiver to pass through me. "This complicates things."

"Possibly."

He smiles. "Why, possibly?"

"Because it depends on what secret you're hiding."

"You think I'm hiding a secret?"

"Aren't you?"

He pulls me even closer and whispers, "Possibly."

Despite everything, I laugh. Will he tell me everything, or will I never know? It doesn't seem to matter at this moment. What does is where we go from here because my heart is on a rollercoaster right now and I'm not sure if I can take another downward dip.

Jake pulls me tight against his side and we head back along the deck, passing several other couples with the same thing in mind.

Jake whispers, "Is that your friend, Ellen?"

I almost daren't look as I spy a couple kissing rather passionately on a nearby deckchair, but luckily it is just someone who looks like her.

"Thankfully, no. You know, I just can't get an image of the three of them in Norman's stateroom out of my head, minus several items of clothing. Do you think we'll be like that when we're older – although, I don't mean together of course?"

"Why not?" He grins. "This could be the start of a beautiful love affair. We could travel the world, learn sixteen languages and find diamonds in the mountains. Then we would set up home on a ranch and raise donkeys. Children would follow, who would grow up to be as amazing as their parents and be the next Bill Gates, or even the Prime Minister. We can do anything, Florrie, as long as we want to."

"You talk the talk, Jake, but by the sounds of it your walk involves a rocky climb."

"Why not. You can do anything you want to in life, you just need to find out how it's done. So, with that in mind, what would you like most in the world?"

His mood is infectious and I think hard. "Lots of things I suppose but one thing more than any other."

"Which is?"

"To be happy."

He stops suddenly and looks concerned. "Why, aren't you happy now?"

"I suppose I am, on the ship, more than happy really, but here we are in a bubble for two weeks, taken out of our normal life for a brief bit of respite. My problems will still be there when I go home. I'm still Florence Monroe, a beautician with not a lot else. I have to start again and that's a daunting task."

"Then don't go home. Be Florence Monroe intrepid explorer. You said yourself you have nothing and need to start again. Why don't you start again in Dream Valley? It's a great place to live and anything's possible there."

"Well, Sammy certainly thinks so."

"See, you already have a best friend there and someone who wants to see a lot more of you."

"Do you Jake?"

I hate that I sound so needy, but I feel that way right now. I need to know if he's serious and not just using me for whatever secret he's hiding.

Once again, he pulls me close and says huskily, "Just trust me, Florrie. I'm the real deal, I promise you that. I have no hidden agenda and no ulterior motive. I'm just a normal guy who has found a girl he rather likes. Someone like him. Someone who appears to want the same things and can put up with his madness. Fate brought us together, and now we must make the glue stick. So, think about it, think about coming home with me."

He kisses me harder this time with a little desperation thrown into the mix, and I really hope with every part of my heart that this is genuine and not just a very clever line from a very clever player.

34

We should have done this religiously every morning. That's exactly what my body is telling me as I try to make it do things it's never even heard about.

Sammy groans as she tries to hold the pose and I regret agreeing to come to the fab abs fitness class so early. 7.30 is still the middle of the night when you've overindulged the night before and the hours all blend into one.

"At least we have breakfast to look forward to."

She grimaces as she tries to hold the plank position and I hiss, "I'd rather be having a lie in if I'm honest. Maybe this wasn't such a good idea."

The alcohol is pouring through my pores as I sweat it out and Sammy grunts, "Well, I'm making it my new regime. How have I let myself go so much; this is torture?"

Beside us woman twice our age are effortlessly moving through the routine without any ill effects it seems and I'm ashamed at my own lack of stamina. In fact, the lesson this is teaching is that I should exercise more and drink less if I want to be as agile as these women when I'm their age – if I reach it that is.

By the time we shower and reach the restaurant, I have a new resolve set in place.

"You know, Sammy, today is the start of the rest of my life. It's only going to be fruit and natural yoghurt for me, possibly a poached egg on gluten free bread. Potentially a protein shake, or oatmeal sprinkled with chia seeds. I'm pretty sure that would do the trick."

Sammy sighs. "But those pancakes look so good. Lashings of maple syrup and wow, they've even rolled out some chocolate sauce today."

"I obviously meant tomorrow." I say hastily, grabbing a plate nestling beside the pancake stack. "I mean, you can't expect me to begin on empty, I need to have some reward for that extreme workout."

"What the one this morning, or the one last night with Jake?"

Sammy winks and I feel my face blushing a deep shade of red. "For your information, the only workout I had last night with Jake, concerned my lips and a rather enthusiastic hoedown on the Cowshed bar."

I help myself to three pancakes, an extra one this morning to cheer myself up after the early rude awakening it had to endure and Sammy laughs. "Hmm, well I'm pleased for you, you deserve a bit of fun, we both do."

She selects her own pancake and liberally sprinkles it with nuts, chocolate and tiny marshmallows which is actually a really good idea so I do the same.

"So, what happened in your world last night? Did you watch the film and then head to bed like you intended?"

"Of course," For some reason she looks a little cagey and I wonder what's going on in her life at the moment.

Luckily, this is a sea day and we have a meeting with Marcus before spending the rest of the day sunbathing and enjoying even more food.

As we walk to his stateroom, Sammy seems a little subdued, so I say tentatively, "Is everything ok, I'm worried about you?"

"Me, why?" She seems genuinely surprised which makes me feel a little better.

"I don't know, you just seem thoughtful and not your usual bubbly self."

"I'm fine." She smiles and links her arm in mine. "I suppose I'm a little overwhelmed with everything. First being here on the cruise after quitting my job. I suppose the reality of that is just sinking in. Then there's this ship, it's a melting pot of emotions and I'm struggling to make sense of mine."

"In what way?"

She smiles faintly, "I've never been so popular and the guys are seriously amazing. Part of me thinks it's a dream and the other part of me thinks it's a nightmare."

"Why a nightmare, the dream bit is obvious, they are gorgeous."

"Because I have a decision to make and can't decide."

"What on your final date for next week? I must say, my mind is made up already."

"Jake, obviously." She laughs. "He's good for you, Florrie. Easy going, good fun and laid back, just what you need right now."

"He's asked me to relocate to Dream Valley."

She stops and stares at me with a stunned expression.

"Since when?"

"Last night. He told me it's an amazing place to live and

because you would be there, and him obviously, I should make the break and start again."

"That's fantastic, please say you will."

"I'm not sure. I mean, it's quite a big step and what if this is just a holiday fling, a sticking plaster over a festering wound? Oliver has been a big part of my life for the past four years and after the trauma of the wedding, I could be in a vulnerable state right now and not thinking straight."

"Does it matter?"

"It does to me."

For a moment, we just walk in silence and Sammy says sadly, "Then we both have the same problem. You know, Florrie, all of this attention is messing with my head. I don't know who and what to believe anymore, so do you know what I'm going to do?"

"Tell me." I am holding onto every word she says because whatever she decides could influence my own decision and she says firmly. "I'm taking the offer of the job, the flat and the new life. On those terms only, nothing else, no romantic attachments, just me and my suitcase starting over. If you like, it has another bedroom and it would be good to share."

I stop suddenly and feel the emotion behind my words as I nod and blink away the sudden surge of tears.

"I would like that, thank you."

"You mean you'll come and start over with me."

"Just try and stop me and for the record, I'm taking a leaf out of your book and doing it on my terms. No romantic attachments just friendship. It's a start at least."

Sammy steps forward and pulls me in for a hug and this is the moment that seals our future.

Dream Valley sounds the perfect place for two confused

women to look for a happily ever after and who better to move forward with than my best friend.

After sealing our deal, we find ourselves standing outside Marcus's stateroom and this time it feels a little different. Now I'm very much part of this new life and I feel excited.

Sammy knocks and it doesn't take long before he opens the door and calls us inside. "Come in, we should make a start, I've got a gym booking I can't be late for."

Just seeing Marcus dressed for the gym makes my mouth water. He is one striking guy and the dark tousled hair, piercing blue eyes and rather toned abs, make me forget my manners as I openly stare at him.

Sammy looks a little worried and I notice the look they share that cuts me out and I wonder about their relationship. There's an undercurrent of something going on and now I'm aware of it, I will make sure I learn what it is sooner rather than later, for Sammy's sake.

"So, all I need you to do is sell this space as if someone is viewing it online. You can use your phones but I have some great equipment on order that will make it easier. Take the viewers through every aspect of the space and demonstrate the good points. Any bad points try to turn into positives."

"How?" I can't imagine any bad points being positive and he shrugs. "I don't know, possibly there are cracks in the walls or the odd visible damp patch. Perhaps the rooms are rather small, like most London flats actually and you need to make the person imagine themselves there. I would start by saying how convenient it is to have everything on hand, less tidying, giving them more time to explore the shops and bars on their doorsteps, not to mention the park nearby and the easy access to theatres and work. There is always a positive to cancel a negative and if they want it badly enough, they will compromise."

He sits on the bed and looks across at Sammy. "Sammy, you start, sell this cabin to me and make me want it more than I've ever wanted anything in my life before."

He beckons me to sit beside him and I watch with interest as she smiles a blinding smile that makes her seem approachable and honest.

"Welcome to this absolutely amazing apartment that has me so excited I can't wait to show you why. First stop has to be the view. Imagine waking up every morning, throwing back the curtains and this is the first thing you see."

She pretends to open the curtains with a flourish and says breathlessly, "Stunning, isn't it? I told you it was amazing. In fact, if I lived here, I would never leave."

She turns and smiles sweetly before moving around the room, pointing out various aspects and demonstrating the space and by the end of it I would buy it myself. I can tell Marcus is impressed because he hasn't taken his eyes off her for a second and a small smile rests on his lips as he watches with admiration.

As she finishes up, I spontaneously applaud and she half curtseys before he says rather gruffly, "Ok, good. Florence it's your turn now."

It feels a little awkward running through an almost identical presentation but it doesn't appear to matter because I could be reciting Shakespeare right now because I get the feeling their attention is elsewhere. Their body language is guarded and there's tension in the room and every word I speak appears to fall short of them actually hearing it.

I even throw in a few French words to test their reactions and they remain iced in their positions, staring blankly in front of them as if they are actually listening to me.

By the time I finish there's an awkward silence and then Marcus nods. "Great, well done, you've both got the hang of this. So, now you know what it involves, have you any questions?"

For the next half an hour we discuss the finer details and at the end of it, Sammy says happily, "Marcus we forgot to say that Florence is relocating to Dream Valley.

"Interesting."

He looks thoughtful and I say hastily, "I hope that's ok, it's just that Sammy mentioned there was a spare room in the flat that comes with the job and well, I could work for you when I'm not building up my business again."

"Your business?"

"Beauty to Go. I'm a mobile beauty technician and can fit the two jobs to work together. I mean, I'm not expecting you to give me a full-time job or anything and I'll pay my rent ..."

"It's ok, Florrie, I'll sort it with Marcus."

Sammy looks at him and once again a silent conversation appears to be taking place and Marcus nods. "Ok, we'll talk about it later. I really need to get to the gym."

Sammy nods and quickly guides me out of his stateroom and as the door closes, I sense I may have been present but I certainly wasn't in the loop. It's obvious there's something happening here and they don't want anyone to find out what it is.

35

Weirdly, today's date is taking part in an activity, pottery painting.

When I reach my table, I'm not surprised to see Brad waiting for me.

"We meet at last, Florence."

He grins as I slip into the seat opposite him, and I nod. "It was only a matter of time."

Catching sight of Sammy Jo across the room, I'm not surprised to see her date is Jake and as he catches my eye, he grins wickedly and points to his arm in the exact place I had my 'property of Jake' tattoo.

Laughing, I turn my attention back to his brother, who is looking at a mug awkwardly. "Why did I choose something without corners, how is this going to work?"

"I take it you've never been pottery painting before then."

"I'm a pottery virgin and I hope I'm paired up with an experienced woman who will guide me through."

He winks suggestively and I roll my eyes as I contemplate my own little keepsake box that I chose from the display on offer.

As we work away, he chats about everything he's done so far and the conversation flows well and easily. He is definitely Jake's brother because he's cheeky, a little crude and the looks he gives you make your cheeks burn and your heart flutter. Whoever taught these guys to flirt knows their stuff, and yet Marcus and Dom appear to be on another level. Brooding, intense with many layers and their personality buried deep inside.

"So, tell me about Jake, any scandal, any embarrassing stories; I'd love to know." I smile as I contemplate my colour choice.

"How long have we got?" He glances across at his brother, who apparently has Sammy in stitches and says thoughtfully, "Jake's a good guy for the most part. Like me, he tends to keep out of family drama and just get on with life. Unfortunately, we have been dragged into this nightmare and like me, he is trying to get through it as best he can."

"You mean your father's death; I was so sorry to hear about that."

"Thanks. It was a shock, but we had time to prepare, so did he as it happens and his decision has made it difficult to focus on anything else."

"Jake tells me it concerns your inheritance. You need to have been married for two years before it's yours. That's a lot of pressure for anyone to bear."

Brad looks surprised. "He told you, I'm shocked."

"Why?"

"Because it's a little weird and may put you off him."

He bites the end of his paintbrush thoughtfully. "Do you

like him, Florence, I mean, could you see a future with him?"

The million-dollar question. I'm not sure how to answer it and as I look across and catch Jake's eye, the smile he sends my way warms my heart.

"What's not to love, he's a great guy, good personality, laid back and rather easy on the eye?"

"Then he's luckier than the rest of us."

"What do you mean?" Brad looks sad and I feel bad for that because the earlier carefree conversation appears to be getting more intense by the second.

"I'm worried that my father got it wrong. Setting us this challenge with the inheritance as a reward. Surely, it's better to let fate and nature takes its course. Forced marriages aren't good for anyone involved. Marcus and Dom are in a race against time and don't care who they trample on to get there. I'm content to wait until they fight it out before making my move and Jake is the lucky one."

"Why?"

He smiles ruefully. "Because out of all of us he has found someone he actually sees a future with and not because of any will. Jake genuinely likes you and I hope for his sake you do too because out of the four of us, if this worked out Jake will be richer than us all."

"Is it just about money then?" A bad feeling washes over me and Brad shakes his head. "Not in his case. Jake's in no hurry which is ironic really when he was the first to find somebody he's interested in."

"What about you, is there nobody in your sights and I'm not talking about this cruising in love thing? I'm a little surprised that none of you have a girlfriend already. Surely there's someone?"

He laughs and a little of his cheekiness returns. "There

are many women, Florence, that's the problem. It's why our father did this in the first place. Where we come from there's a line at the door and we are moving along it."

"That's disgusting."

"I agree." He winks. "But when you're the one with the pick of the crop, it's too tempting to ignore."

"And Jake." I feel my heart go into free-fall. "Does he move along the line too?"

"Not really." He smiles encouragingly. "Jake is more in love with himself and his business than anyone else. He's not interested in dating, or so I thought."

He picks up his mug and I have to laugh because it's a real disaster. He's painted it some kind of sludgy brown/yellow colour and tried to write his name on it that any four-year-old could have done a better job.

"I don't think I'm an artist; yours looks good though. Can we swap?"

Looking at my little trinket box that I have painted pink with contrasting pink love hearts all around it, I raise my eyes. "Really, you want your brothers to think you painted this?"

He shrugs. "It would make a nice gift for my mum. She would place it on the mantlepiece in pride of place, knowing I had made it. Mums are like that, you know."

Thinking of my own art collection through the ages that now lives on several shelves dotted around the house, I tend to agree with him.

Pushing it across the table, I smile. "Then it's yours. It will be our secret."

Brad nods and then says in a strangely wistful voice, "Then you will fit in perfectly with our family, Florence. Secrets should be our middle name."

It doesn't take long for Jake and Sammy to head over and

proudly show us their own works of art. Jake has also painted a mug with 'number one game player' written on the side, and Brad catches my eye with a knowing, 'I told you so' look.

Sammy Jo has decorated a small candle holder much the same as me with little love hearts, although hers is a chic light grey.

As we head off, we decide to chill for a while and grab a coffee on deck and it feels nice sharing time with people who are fun and easy going. The trouble is, Brad's conversation is raising red flags because if they are guarding secrets, I may not like what happens when they are revealed.

~

After a while the guys head off to enjoy the speed climbing wall and we start walking to the towel folding demonstration before lunch.

As we walk, she links her arm in mine and says happily, "You know, I really like Jake, he's perfect for you."

"I know."

"Good looking, funny and intelligent and just wow if his project comes off."

"What project?" I stop in my tracks and sense she's a little uncomfortable. "Oh, didn't he tell you? I'm sorry I didn't know it was a secret."

Suddenly, I feel as if I'm faced with an impenetrable wall of secrets on every side of me and I suppose this is the final straw because I say firmly, "Ok, as soon as we have learned how to fold a towel into a swan, I want to know everything, Sammy. You have something bothering you, Jake has a secret, the whole Hudson family appear to be one big secret and if there's one thing I can't deal with right now, is more people I love holding some kind of catastrophic secret from me that is sure to blow up in my face when I least expect it."

Sammy Jo looks so guilty I know I'm right and as she opens her mouth to speak, we hear a firm, "Sammy Jo."

Spinning around, we see Marcus looking at Sammy with a dark expression, and she shuts down immediately. Whatever she was about to say remains unspoken as she nods. "Hey, Marcus, where are you heading?"

"To find you actually, I wondered if you had a moment."

"Well..." She looks at me apologetically, and I shrug.

"It's fine. I'm not that interested in towel origami, anyway. I could work on my tan instead if you need a minute."

Sammy looks torn, but there's something about the commanding way Marcus has about him that beats her down and she nods. "Thanks. I catch up with you at lunch. Is one o'clock, ok?"

"Sure, see you then."

I watch them head off and note they don't share a word and I'm almost tempted to shadow them and spy on my friend. Instead, I head to our stateroom to change for an hour of lapping up the sun and wonder if I'll ever get to the bottom of what on earth is going on?

36

Lunch is rather rushed and Sammy Jo seems preoccupied. Unfortunately, we have to share our table with Mandy and Simon who are full of everything they've done so far and we listen with interest to their tales of a very different experience to ours. Watching them laugh at each other's comments and the way they share intimate looks and personal jokes makes me long for that kind of relationship myself. If Oliver was here with me now, would we be that couple? Part of me insists we would, but there's the part of me with common sense that tells me we were never that couple in the first place.

It upsets me to think I ever thought we were. Maybe at the beginning, but that initial spark soon extinguished and never really caught the flame to burn steadily and brightly. We were swept along on what we thought was the right thing to do and now I know Oliver was completely right to end it, although I can never forgive him for the catastrophic way he went about it.

Picturing Jake beside me, I can see a future like that with

him. But am I looking at it through rose-coloured spectacles?

Do we really know?

Do we really find that perfect man who was always meant for us or do we settle for one who ticks most of the boxes?

Brad's words make me feel a little better because at least Jake doesn't appear to be playing a game, unlike the rest of them. And my friend, how is she caught up in this because the more I think about it, I know there is something bothering her and she's struggling to cope?

After eating enough to feed a small family for a week, we head off to the 'increase your metabolism' seminar, and I tentatively broach the subject as we walk.

"Regarding what I said earlier, about the secrets, you know you can tell me anything, right?"

"Of course."

"Is it Marcus, is he making you do something you're unhappy about because if he is, you don't have to take that job you know?"

"Marcus." She stops and looks at me in surprise. "No, Marcus has been nothing short of amazing. To be honest, I'm so glad I met him, he's certainly opened my eyes."

"Then what is it?" I'm a little surprised because I had him down as some kind of Bond Villain and she sighs heavily. "If you must know, I'm struggling with this cruising in love programme. We have to make our choice in a couple of days and I'm not sure I can."

"Why not? I know you have endless choices but surely one of them stands out more than the other."

"Maybe, but there's no way I can agree to spend my week with any of them?"

"Why not?" I am so confused right now, and she sighs.

"It doesn't matter. I'll work it out. What about you, I'm guessing Jake is number 1-7 on your list?"

"You would be right."

"I'm pleased for you, Florrie. Jake is one thousand times better than Oliver. It's funny how things work out, isn't it? I mean, there you were a week ago, broken hearted and with no prospects..."

"I wouldn't put it quite like that." I laugh nervously, and she grins. "Ok then, alone and at a turning point in your life. Well, now you have a great guy beside you, a new job if you want it and a great flatmate."

"Obviously." We share a giggle and a little of the cloud lifts and she appears to regain her light spirit. "Come on, let's go and learn how to stay forever slim while eating junk food for the rest of our lives; I can't afford to miss this."

Once again she swerved my probing and once again, I let it go because one thing I do know is that Sammy Jo will tell me when she's good and ready. Although I just hope it's not too late that I can't change her mind.

~

I'M NOT sure I can breathe because I have never laughed so much in my life. Jake, Brad, and Sammy Jo have joined me in the flash mob dancing class and along with about fifty other passengers, we are currently working through a programme of songs that are more at home in the movies. Our small part of this involves us belting out Aufwiedersehn goodbye, while doing some kind of Irish jig. Cruise ship Bobby is overseeing the whole operation and even Ellen and Geoffrey can be seen tango dancing on the lower deck with the over sixties strictly ballroom challenge team.

It's hard to believe that any of us have troubles to deal with as we dance and sing our way into happiness.

Following the extreme workout, Brad disappears off on a mysterious date, and Sammy makes her excuses before I can ask where she's going.

"Alone at last." Jake slips his arm around my waist and kisses me sweetly on the top of my head. "Fancy a cocktail, babe, I heard today's special is porn star martini and I'm liking the sound of that."

"Sounds amazing."

We walk towards the piano bar and it feels nice with his arm resting lightly across my shoulders and I love the warm smiles directed our way by older couples and various staff members. It's like we are one big ship-sized family and I can't imagine wanting to holiday any other way in the future.

As soon as we are tucked into a booth sipping cocktails while staring into each other's eyes, I try to find the answers I am desperate for.

"Sammy told me about your exciting project, you must be happy."

He looks a little surprised. "She told you then."

"Hm," I take a sip from my cocktail, hoping he doesn't ask me the finer details because then I would have to confess I know nothing.

He grins and looks extremely excited. "To be honest, Florrie, I was kind of hoping to tell you towards the end of the week, when I got to know you a bit better."

"But you told Sammy Jo." I feel a little hurt by that and he leans forward and kisses my lips, slowly and with a delicious sense of ownership.

Pulling back, he whispers, "I just wanted to make you fall in love with me first."

A small tingle starts deep in my soul and works its way to my heart because I have a feeling that would be the easy part. I could definitely see myself falling hopelessly in love with this man and yet for some reason he needs to keep something from me first. "Are you testing my loyalty, then?"

He nods. "A little, but I don't know why. Maybe because I want to see if you like me for me and not what's around the corner."

"I can't see around corners, Jake and if you must know, I like you for who you are. I don't know you, not really. I don't know your taste in music, your hobbies, your life history and any annoying little habits you have that I would hate. It's possible we don't share the same dreams, taste in food or anything. We may be incompatible in every way but I'm kind of looking forward to finding that out. Isn't that what happens? Attraction first and then discovering the person inside. Well, so far so good and whatever secret you're hiding, won't change how I feel now."

To my surprise, he pulls me close and kisses me harder, deeper, and more passionately than before. It takes my breath away and when he releases me, the flush on my face is not because of the cocktail.

"Then I'll tell you."

He looks at me with a serious expression and I hold my breath in anticipation of one more puzzle piece sliding into place.

"It's my business, it's about to do rather well."

"That's good, isn't it?"

I feel happy for him and he nods, the light sparkling in his eyes as he says with enthusiasm. "I've been working on a game, you know, computers. It's been years of planning and I finally finished it. Before I came on this trip, I had a meeting with a manufacturer and I received the email signing it up two days ago."

"That's amazing, congratulations." I feel happy for him because he looks so proud and his delight is catching.

"So, when we return, I can quit my job and work on it full time. I finally have my own company and don't need to work in an IT department losing the will to live. Marcus is setting me up with an office and I'm going to be working from home in Dream Valley."

He takes my hand. "Life is working out rather well for me as it happens and I suppose I held back because my feelings for you may scare you away."

He looks worried, and I smile to reassure him.

"I'm keen to see where this goes too, Jake, but slowly, so let's not rush into anything and just take it one step at a time. It sounds good though, you should be proud of yourself."

He nods, looking thoughtful. "You know, Florrie, I never really expected my business to succeed. It always seemed like a pipe-dream. You know, things like this happen to other people, not me. I've always wanted to have a shot at seeing my game out on the market but never really expected it. This just shows that anything is possible and if you have a good idea and put the work in, learn the business and take a few risks, anything could happen. I think that could apply to us as well."

"In what way?" I hold my breath because Jake seems so serious, which is completely unlike him and as he takes my hand, I feel my life shifting once again.

"Then I met you. A woman who should never have been sitting here with me, destined for another. I shouldn't be here, but fate has intervened and here we both are. Now you are coming home with me, although for a very different reason. A new life and a new dream from the one you thought you wanted and we have a chance to see where this takes us. I'm hoping you spend the next week with me and like what you see and I'll be on my best behaviour because I don't want to scare you away."

"Don't."

He looks confused and I smile. "Don't be on your best behaviour, Jake, I want to see the real you. I'm pretty certain I'm going to like him a lot, but for now that's all this will be. A time to grow, to learn about one another and when we step off this ship, we have a chance of continuing this – friendship, back on dry land. Let's make no promises or declarations and just enjoy getting to know one another."

"That's fine with me." Jake lifts my hand to his lips and kisses it sweetly, and then grins. "So, are you up for the dodge ball competition, or karaoke? I'm good with either."

"I was hoping to attend the 'how to tell if your partner is a spy' seminar. I'd really hate to miss it."

"Then lead on Moneypenny, this could be interesting."

37

It feels a little pointless meeting my final date the next morning. Cruise ship Bobby has arranged an alfresco breakfast on the sundeck for the final contenders and it looks lovely with the plump cushions set around the white metal tables, with white parasols casting shade onto the jugs of brightly coloured juice and fresh fruit cocktails. I have chosen to wear a simple white sundress that complements my growing suntan, and I feel like a movie star as I perch my shades on the top of my head and look with interest at my final date.

"Well, this is a nice surprise."

I beam as I see a familiar face smiling back at me.

"It seems like ages since we first met. How have you been, Florrie?"

"Good thanks, how about you?"

Ben is looking quite dashing in a white polo shirt and navy shorts, and his tan is even more impressive than mine. In fact, he looks super-cool as he leans back in his chair and lifts the glass of juice to his lips.

"I've had an amazing time, met some great people and really chilled out. How about you?"

"Same. You know, I was quite reluctant to sign up for this dating thing but it has really opened my eyes."

He nods. "I agree. I've met quite a few shockers actually, some good and one in particular I'm keen to spend more time with."

I'm interested to hear who, and he grins.

"Her name's Lucy, and she's on holiday with a group of friends. To be honest, she's the most normal one out of a bad bunch, present company aside of course."

"Of course." I look around and see Sammy chatting away to a man who looks much older than her and Ben says, "I hear your friend has been in demand."

"Hm, what did you hear?"

"Lucy told me she's had a few dates with guys who mentioned her. Apparently, there's some kind of competition going on and I'm not sure whether to feel sorry for her, or congratulate her."

"Why?"

He leans forward and whispers, "Lucy told me one of her dates couldn't take his eyes off your friend the whole time she was on a date with another guy. When she asked if he knew her, the guy seemed a little tense and said that she was the only girl he was interested in and if his brothers would just back off, he would make it his mission to get her to choose him. Lucy questioned him on it, and he changed the subject. I must say, your friend has quite a choice to make because it appears the ball is in her court."

I shrug, "Yes, she has got caught up in some kind of family feud and hopefully tomorrow will put an end to it because we still have a week to go and I'm not sure my nerves can take it."

We tuck into our food and it feels nice spending uncomplicated time with a man who appears to be enjoying the experience. We chat about the places we've been, things we've done on the ship and swapped suggestions and warned against things that weren't worth the time.

When we part company, I'm relieved this is over because now I can concentrate on getting to know Jake without the dates getting in the way.

When Ben leaves, Sammy Jo takes his place and sighs. "Thank God it's over, that man was seriously creepy."

"In what way, he seemed quite nice?"

"Not really. He spent the whole time trying to get me to sign up to his modelling agency. He told me he could 'audition' me in the cabin at 2 pm and could fit me in between dates number 3 and 5.

"Are you kidding me?"

She starts to laugh. "I wish I was. Apparently, he gets all his 'models' this way and is a regular on the cruising in love programme on whatever ship he can get on. He was so businesslike, Flo. I mean, he asked me if I had any friends and we could audition together. When I questioned what the audition involved, he told me to bring a bikini and strike a few poses on his balcony."

"Were you tempted?"

"Absolutely not." She laughs. "It was when he told me the real money was in glamour modelling that I really tuned out. He was quite enthusiastic telling me all about the wonders of the internet and how his models were making hundreds and thousands of pounds from their own bedrooms by paid subscriptions. He really tried to make it sound legit and like a job at the checkouts, or working as a receptionist. He gave me his card and said if I don't show up to cabin 1250 at 2 o'clock, he would have his answer but feel free to pass it on to anyone who may be interested."

Spying Ellen and Geoffrey walking past, I grab the card and wink. "I know someone who would definitely be interested. Follow me."

Giggling, we head out on deck and Ellen beams as she sees us heading towards her. "Darlings, my two favourite singles on the prowl. What have you got for me?"

Sammy grins as I present her with the card. "An opportunity, actually."

Ellen almost snatches it from my hand. "What is it? I hope it's something interesting because I'm feeling in dire need of some spice in my life."

By the time we finish filling her in, she looks both horrified and excited at the same time.

Turning to Geoffrey, she grins. "I think we should pay this gentleman a visit, don't you?"

Geoffrey laughs. "Of course we should. He sounds like that guy from Stoke-on-Trent we met on the Allura. Do you remember, he was escorted from the ship when we docked in Mexico?"

Ellen nods. "Yes, he was running a porn site from his laptop and getting women to unknowingly star in his movies, while he beamed it live to the internet. Such a fun cruise, I wonder what happened to him?"

Sammy nudges me sharply in the ribs, and I stare at the couple in utter astonishment. "Did that really happen?"

"Oh, I could tell you worse stories than that, my dear. The trouble is, the cruise just isn't long enough to relay them all. Yes, once you've experienced a cruise you never go back because no other holiday provides quite the same excitement, not to mention the entertainment, isn't that right Geoffrey?"

"Spot on, Ellen. Now sorry to cut in on the conversation but we really should prepare ourselves for geriatric scuba diving."

"Is it that time already, goodness doesn't time fly when you're having fun?"

They head off and Sammy laughs so hard the tears run down her face.

"I would love to see them in a wetsuit. Maybe we should go and watch."

"Do you think they actually dive or just watch a film on it, I just can't see Ellen getting her hair wet?"

"To be honest, I've changed my mind. The last thing I want imprinted on my memory is the sight of Geoffrey in a wetsuit. Come on, let's go and grab a sun bed, I really need to chill out."

Sammy grabs my hand and we head off, hopefully for a quiet session by the pool.

38

Tonight, is the 'Aphrodite in White' grand party which marks the halfway point of the cruise. We are so excited about this because at some point in the proceedings, cruise ship Bobby will reveal our final match based on the requests we handed in after the last date.

Tomorrow we dock in Antigua and the idea is to make that the first date with your chosen one and then it's up to you to make it work. As I already know my choice has also chosen me, I am just looking forward to spending a lovely week getting to know Jake on this super ship and if there is any cloud on my horizon, it's that my friend appears to be in a predicament.

She is unusually quiet as we get ready, which is unlike her because she usually sings in the shower and causes a great deal of mess as she decides on the best look for the evening. Tonight is different though and I try to get her to open up, but she just smiles and says she'll tell me later.

Despite her strange mood, Sammy Jo looks excited when we spray our perfume and leave the stateroom in a –

state, actually. It's always the same and it could really do with a tidy up and I dread anyone seeing how messy we are. There is make-up on every surface and abandoned clothes on the floor and discarded bottles and glasses in dire need of a wash. The bed is unmade and the wet towels are in a crumpled heap in the corner. It's just easier to shut my eyes and forget about it and as the door closes behind us, I make a silent vow to clean up my act as well as my love life and become a super woman in every way.

"Do you think there's some kind of Martha Stewart or Mrs Hinch seminar on this ship?" I say in despair.

Sammy laughs. "If there is, we could certainly do with a couple of tickets. It doesn't bode well for our flat sharing, does it?"

"Not really." I laugh and link my arm with my friend, who looks stunning in a white maxi dress with her hair curled on top of her head, making her look like the goddess Aphrodite herself.

My own choice of a white silk pantsuit is not a look I usually go for but I'm happy with my choice and my own chestnut hair is curled and hangs long down my back. I don't miss the appreciative looks thrown our way as we pass several men who are dressed immaculately for the first formal occasion on board.

There's a different kind of atmosphere tonight. Excitement mixed with enthusiasm for an evening filled with cocktails, good food and dancing until the early hours.

"Are you worried about the selection reveal later?" I look at my friend with interest because she hasn't mentioned it once, making me feel as if she knows the outcome already.

"A little, are you?"

"Not really. I think Jake has picked me but there's a small part of me that wonders if fate has somehow messed it up and paired me with Norman or someone equally unsuitable."

Sammy laughs. "I can't see that happening but it would be funny to watch."

"No, it wouldn't." I shiver with revulsion and she laughs. "I wonder what unlucky girl/woman will get the short straw with him. I would certainly pull out if it was me."

"Can you do that, pull out I mean?"

"Of course. It's a holiday after all. If you don't want to spend the last week of it with someone you'd rather not, how can they stop you?"

"I suppose." We make our way to the Crystal bar and I say quickly, "How about you, Sammy? You never did tell me who you chose. Who is the lucky guy?"

"Sammy." We hear someone calling her name and as we look around, I'm surprised to see her unrequited love, Joseph bearing down on us. I feel her tense beside me and look on in astonishment as he stops just short of us and seems a little worried.

"Hi." He appears lost for words and Sammy says in a strained voice, "Hi, Joseph."

For a moment it feels a little awkward and then he says nervously, "I, um, don't suppose you have a minute, um, in private."

She nods and says apologetically, "Do you mind. Florrie, I promise I won't be long."

"It's fine." I spy a $10 sale going on in a shop nearby and say quickly, "I'll be in there. Make sure you don't leave me too long though because I'm out of control when there's a sale."

"Promise." She heads off with Joseph, and I sigh. Great, another problem thrown into the mix at the last minute. Oh, to have her problems.

As I look at the bargains on offer, I'm quite glad about the free time because some of these are a steal. I select some lovely bracelets and a silk scarf that matches a stylish white leather look handbag that I simply must have. By the time I finish, I have acquired at least $50 worth of bargains and congratulate myself on saving what must surely be a small fortune.

The only trouble is, I have to return to my cabin to leave them there and so I dash off a quick text to Sammy and tell her I'll meet her in the Crystal bar and head off back to the cabin to add to the mess we left behind.

On the way I spy Marcus and Dom apparently having a rather heated discussion by the fountain, and I drag my heels a little as I draw near, ducking behind a nearby pillar in a shameless act of eavesdropping.

The only thing I can make out is an angry hiss from Dom, who is looking as if he wants to punch the smug look off Marcus's face as he growls, "If you think this changes anything you're mistaken and if you go ahead, I'll never forgive you."

I jump when I feel a warm kiss planted on the back of my neck, and as I spin around, I am pulled tightly against a familiar chest. "Caught in the act."

The husky drawl makes me smile as I stare rather guiltily into Jake's eyes. "I don't know what you mean?" I try to look innocent and he whispers, "You should take up espionage, it suits you."

"Maybe I will. I'm sure there's a seminar on it in a few days' time."

Grinning, he says quickly, "Let me help you with those necessities."

Rolling his eyes, he prises the bags from my hand and says, "So, where were you off to before you got distracted?"

"My cabin. I was side tracked by a sale and need to deposit my shopping."

"I'll help you."

We head back the way I came and Jake says brightly, "So, the moment of truth will soon be revealed. Just so you know, I made you my number one to seven. I didn't give any other choice."

It feels good to hear that and I feel happy as I anticipate a whole week of getting to know a man who is fast turning out to be my perfect match.

"Same." For a minute we just grin at one another and almost forget we are surrounded by excited passengers looking to party.

It feels good walking beside him, and I wonder if that feeling will change back in Dream Valley. Almost as if he can read my mind, although I did notice there was a seminar on that a few days ago and wouldn't put it past him to have been in the front row, he says, "You'll love Dream Valley, Florrie, it's a special place."

"Tell me about it."

I'm interested to hear about a place I've foolishly agreed to call home, and he smiles. "I've lived all my life in Dream Valley and couldn't think of a better place to live. The countryside is amazing, and is set close to a white sandy beach that's surrounded by crystal blue water. There is a small village with the usual local shops, although if my brother has his way it won't stay that way for long."

"Which brother?"

"Marcus." He shakes his head and sighs.

"It's been driving a wedge through the heart of our family. Like my father, Marcus is ambitious, and his property empire is only starting to grow. The business has distorted his vision and made him hungry for more and it appears that our father shared his vision."

"What vision?"

"Dream Valley is a rough diamond. A paradise that has been protected by my family for generations. Most of it is tied up in trust and now, with my father's death, it's unlocked pandora's box."

We reach my cabin and as we venture inside, he laughs out loud.

"Wow, this place is something else. I thought we were messy but you take the trophy."

"It's Sammy, what can I say, that woman's a mess in every way."

I hold my breath and count to ten as I throw my friend under the bus because I can't have Jake thinking of me as anything other than perfect, and he grins.

"Keep telling yourself that babe."

He wanders over to the balcony doors and opens them, letting the cool night breeze filter through the room and as we step outside onto the balcony, it feels natural to lean on the rail and look at the starry sky. It's so nice standing side by side as we listen to gentle lapping of the waves as the ship cuts its path through to the next port of paradise.

"So, I'm sure you will soon discover what that box contains, probably tonight and so I'll prepare you for the bombshell my brother's about to explode."

My heart starts beating a little faster as I sense that somehow my friend will be caught up in that explosion, and he sighs.

"I wasn't entirely truthful with you when I told you about the inheritance."

Wondering if I have time to grab a vodka out of the mini

bar, I prepare myself for the shattering of my delusional dream.

"My father was a conniving master player, which is probably why he did so well in life and not something I aspire to be. He didn't care whose life he trampled over to get what he wanted and made many difficult decisions without a care, it seemed. Marcus and Dom are the same. Both of them only interested in wealth, power and a future many could only dream about."

He sighs. "Like me, Brad is content to go with the flow. Just try to get by doing what we love, even if it doesn't bring us the same financial rewards, although luckily for me, my business is set to earn me a nice lifestyle if it works out."

I feel happy for him because people like Jake deserve their good fortune.

"You've worked hard for this, and from what I understand when everyone else was lining up to date half the village, you were content with developing your business idea."

"Who told you that?" He seems surprised and then laughs when I say, "Brad."

"I thought so. Brad is the worst one of us all. He's had more girls than I've had breakfast and I never miss that." Shaking his head, he stares out at the night sky and groans. "I'm sorry about my two older brothers. They are caught up in a war that will leave them both bloodied and bruised in the end and Dream Valley will be the casualty."

"What are they planning?"

I feel worried for Jake and his family and he shrugs. "As I said, my father made conditions in his will. We will only receive our inheritance when we marry, or if we have kids we get it sooner. I wasn't lying when I told you it suited me and I was happy to wait because what I want is the last thing on offer. So, as it turns out, I have to wait for my three brothers to marry and receive theirs before mine is up for grabs."

"What do you want then?"

It all sounds like a film script and he says proudly. "My father was a solid investor. He bought shares in almost everything and did well out of it. The portfolio he has is impressive and aside from the fact it would set me up for life, it's something that interests me. His estate was divided into four parts, the investments being the final prize up for grabs. So, now you see I have the easy task of waiting for my brothers to stake their claims to what they want most and then claiming mine when the dust settles."

"But what if they don't – marry that is? Your father's fortune could be tied up for years. How is that good for anyone?"

"Because it's still held in trust. It will be overseen by a board of trustees, as it always has been. That's what the row is about. Marcus and Dom want the first prize and are likely to cause problems in getting it."

"What is the first one?"

I am so interested in finding out what other secrets this family is holding because as secrets go, theirs are more interesting than most.

"The first one is the house and all its land. Marcus wants to take control of that and develop it."

"That's terrible, it's your home."

"The house is the smallest part of the land. It's an estate consisting of several thousand acres of farmland, woodland and estate housing. I mentioned before that my mother will relocate to one of the lodges. Well, Marcus wants to develop the rest into a small town which will make Dream Valley a much busier place to live. He intends on building a school, several houses and a small community, greatly enlarging the one we have."

"Wow, I'm guessing the locals aren't too happy about that."

"I don't think they even know of his plans. I mean, don't get me wrong, ever since my father died, there have been rumours. All his life he protected the land from people like Marcus and now they have to deal with the enemy within."

"And Dom, is that why he's so keen to pursue Sammy Jo, to secure his inheritance."

I feel so angry for my friend and Jake sighs. "It appears so. He realised that she was the perfect candidate, and there was the added bonus of liking her as well. I suppose he thought he had it in the bag and then Marcus happened."

"So, he plans on asking her to marry him to secure the property. This a disaster for Sammy Jo, do you think she knows?"

"Knowing both of them, I'd say it's likely. What do you think she'll do?"

"I'm not sure." However, I know my friend and she's in a vulnerable position right now and is likely to do something rash, so it's important I get to her before she makes a decision she will regret for the rest of her life.

Turning to Jake, I say with determination. "We should go and find her before it's too late."

He looks worried and as we make our way back to the Crystal bar, I just hope she hasn't done anything stupid.

39

The room is packed and amid a sea of white gowns and tuxedos, I frantically search for my friend.

It's only when I see cruise ship Bobby dressed in his officer's uniform, I know I'm heading in the right direction.

"There you are." He beams as we head towards him and Imogen, looking equally splendid in a matching uniform. "It looks as if you've made your decision already." She looks pointedly at Jake's hand clasping mine, and Bobby looks at his clipboard anxiously.

Then he smiles and with a flourish crosses a line through our names and winks. "The programme triumphs again it seems. Two perfectly matched people who can now enjoy a leisurely week getting to know one another. I love my job."

"Have you seen my friend Sammy; has she been paired up already?" I feel on edge as Bobby looks down at his list and shakes his head in disapproval. "She was one of my retirees I'm afraid."

"What do you mean?" My voice is high as it usually is

when I'm anxious and he sighs. "Some people fail to find their perfect match and pull out of the programme. Your friend came to see me earlier and told me she had already found somebody she wanted to spend the next week with and was sorry for any inconvenience. I must say I was disappointed because she was number one for most people. Such a popular candidate and yet how can I be angry when she has obviously found someone she likes?"

"Or had an offer she couldn't refuse." I hiss to Jake and he nods, looking worried.

"Maybe we should find her and see what's happening."

Excusing ourselves from our gracious hosts, we head off to find Sammy Jo and bump into Ellen and Geoffrey, who look very regal. Ellen is wearing a huge white ballgown that is encrusted with fake diamonds, at least I think they are, nothing would surprise me with Ellen and she even has a sparkling tiara tucked into her updo. Geoffrey is squeezed into a tuxedo that looks two sizes too small for him given the trouser bottoms stop at his ankles and the sleeves just below the elbow.

Ellen beams when she sees Jake's hand in mine and says happily, "Cupid's arrow has struck I see, congratulations."

Jakes slides his arm around my waist and pulls me close by his side and smiles. "I was lucky to find Florence. We should have a great week ahead."

"Yes, the fun is only just beginning as they say." Ellen couldn't appear any happier and I say quickly, "Have you seen Sammy Jo anywhere, I appear to have lost her?"

Geoffrey nods. "I saw her heading to the Starlight rooms. She was with a rather dashing man by her side who appeared very pleased with himself. Then again, he had every reason to, she is an impressive companion for any man."

Ellen nods. "They looked so good together; you have both done well, I feel like a proud mother."

We quickly make our excuses and head off to the Starlight rooms in urgent haste, and as we reach the impressive conference sized room, I see Sammy Jo standing with Jake's brothers looking a little tense.

As we approach, I notice Dom's furious expression and Brad's worried one as Marcus stands holding Sammy Jo's hand, looking like he's won gold at the Olympics. However, that's not the most shocking thing I can see right now because as my eyes are drawn to their clasped hands, I see the biggest diamond I have ever seen sparkling on Sammy's engagement finger.

They all look up when we approach and she must register the horror in my eyes because she says quickly, "Excuse me, I just need a word with Florence."

She moves quickly and pulls me away from the group and guides us to the moonlit deck outside.

"Please tell me that's not what I think it is, Sammy."

Every red flag in existence is waving around her right now as she nods, looking worried.

"I'm sorry, Florrie, I was sworn to secrecy." She holds up her finger and smiles wistfully at the diamond on the third finger of her left hand.

"Are you angry?"

"No, why would I be angry?" I smile weakly. "Just worried. I was afraid this was going to happen and you would be pulled into this family feud."

"It's for the best."

We lean over the rail as is becoming customary and she sighs. "The thing is, Flo, I'm exhausted by it all. Not just this week and the games the guys have been playing but by life actually, my life to be precise."

"Why, you have an amazing life stretching out in front of you. You're still young. Why are you so worried?"

"Because I lack direction and I don't have a plan and things are passing me by. You see, I've always drifted along telling myself that things will work out in the end. That amazing job I always wanted will somehow materialise and I'll be set for life. The man of my dreams will appear one day and sweep me off my feet and everything will slot into place like it's supposed to."

"It will, you just need to give it time."

"Do I, or is *this* that time? I mean, you've met Marcus, what's not amazing about that man? My only worry was you."

"Me! Why are you worried about me?"

"Because you liked him. I thought..."

"I don't." I quickly add, "Maybe before I met Jake, but when he came along, I only saw him. I admit Marcus is one impressive man, but he's also an ambitious one. He's using you Sammy, to get what he wants."

"I know." She shrugs. "Maybe I'm using him too for the same reasons, you see, Florence, Marcus made me an offer I would be a fool to refuse and I've decided to take him up on it."

"Which is?" I kind of know already but want to hear her voice the shallow reason she has agreed to this loveless, conniving, calculated engagement.

"Marcus told me that if we marry for two years, he will set me up for life. A business arrangement that will secure my future and then leave me free to find happiness with another."

"That's cold." I am so worried about my friend and she shrugs. "Maybe, but the trouble is..."

She breaks off and I see the tears glistening in her eyes. "I like him."

"Yes, you've said that already but like doesn't form a marriage contract, it forms a whole heap of trouble in the future. Don't do this, Sammy, it's not worth it."

"But what if I think it is? What if I've well…"

Suddenly, reality hits and I stare at her in shock. "You like him, as in more than like him. Oh, Sammy, I'm so sorry."

She sniffs. "I didn't mean to fall so hard. I was kind of holding back at first and just thought he was going to be my new boss. Then we started spending time together and I know why he was so charming, attentive and funny. He was trying to persuade me to marry him. I'm not a fool. I know what his intentions are. The trouble is, I liked it and I like him and so when he asked, I jumped at the chance because now I have two years to make him fall in love with me."

"Please don't do this Sammy, you'll get hurt."

"Probably, but I owe it to myself to try at least." She sighs heavily. "Then there's Dom."

"What about him?" I definitely have a headache coming on as she shrugs. "He was so insistent and relentless in doing the same as Marcus. It's only when Joseph took me aside and warned me against them that I found out about this plan at all."

"Joseph!" Now I really do have a headache, possibly a migraine, as the horizon swims before my eyes.

"Yes, he told me he overheard them at the dodge ball competition. They were arguing and Dom told him that he would have me over his dead body and that if anyone was going to claim the inheritance, it was him. That he would do everything in his power to make me fall in love with him and Marcus's plans would never make it to the planning committee. Apparently, Marcus was angry and told him he should be ashamed of himself and he would do everything in his power to stop him, for my sake more than the plans he has."

"He said that." I'm surprised and watch as a faraway look enters her eyes and she smiles. "Joseph told me that Marcus said he liked me, really liked me and he wouldn't let his brother ruin my life and any agreement we would have would be in my best interests."

"Admirable." I roll my eyes because knowing Marcus, he was just playing a trump card in the hope it would reach her ears and my friend is so infatuated she fell for it. "But what about Joseph, a few days ago you thought he was the one who got away? Why is he so interested all of a sudden?"

"He's not, he's just being a friend. If anything, seeing him again has helped me make up my mind. For years now I've regretted never having a chance with him and I suppose I've built up his image into one that many can't rise above. Then I met him again and well, let's just say that image doesn't live up to the reality."

She laughs softly. "There was nothing there and I no longer saw him in that way. He seemed quite ordinary really, and was just a fond memory of a happy time. If anything, I feel foolish having spent years pining after something that would have fizzled out and died, sooner rather than later. He did me a favour really and by the sounds of it has met his perfect match anyway and I'm happy for him. He was right to warn me though and I will always be grateful to him for that, but my heart has other plans from my head and I need to try at least. If Marcus doesn't fall in love with me before two years is out, then at least I'll be financially rewarded for my broken heart. That's why I agreed to his indecent proposal because this is one opportunity, one chance of love, that I won't let slip away."

Even though I completely understand the reasons behind her decision, I am so worried about my friend. If anything, my decision to relocate to Dream Valley is now definite because if she is going to go down this path, then I am running along behind her, ready to catch her when she falls.

Yes, Sammy Jo has reached a decision and so have I. Dream Valley is about to get two new residents and the Hudson brothers had better watch out because if they mess up, they will have me to deal with.

40

We head back to the Starlight rooms and I notice the sweet smile Marcus throws her as he reaches for her hand. He's a good actor, I'll give him that and watch as he pulls a bottle of champagne from the ice bucket on the table nearby and fills six glasses.

Handing one to each of us, he raises his glass and stares almost lovingly into Sammy Jo's eyes.

"Now you all know that Sammy Jo has agreed to marry me and make me the happiest man alive."

He kisses her hand and I feel empty inside. This is all a charade; on his part at least, and how can I be happy about that? The trouble is, my friend is more than happy about it as she gazes at him with undisguised emotion and as he raises his glass to her, he says almost lovingly, "Thank you, Sammy Jo, from the bottom of my heart. I can't wait to marry you."

"Oh, for goodness' sake, this is seriously messed up." Dom sets his glass down angrily and glares at his brother, who narrows his eyes. "Sammy Jo, think hard before you commit yourself to a man who is using you to get what he wants. Don't do this and walk away before he ruins your life."

Dom stares at her with the look of a condemned man pleading for forgiveness, and she smiles. "It's ok, we both have our reasons for this marriage and I'm fine with that. Marcus is everything I hoped I'd find, and I'm looking forward to being his wife. If you think it's for his inheritance, then you don't know me at all and I'll look forward to proving you all wrong."

She smiles at Marcus who looks so proud it almost makes me think he feels something for her at least and she says sweetly, "To us, Marcus and our amazing future together."

It feels a little awkward watching a scene that to everyone else is the stuff of fairy tales but we know there's a wicked ending to this one and as Dom storms away and Brad follows him anxiously, Jake and I make polite conversation in a show of solidarity that feels decidedly misplaced.

If I was a stranger looking in from the outside, I would admire the happy couple who appear to have everything going for them. They look good, seem happy and look as if they've found the holy grail but I'm worried for my friend because as men go, Marcus appears more ruthless than most and then there's his brother who is holding my hand and throwing me sweet looks that make me shiver. Is he really being honest with me and how do I feel about his own secret? He won't be asking me to marry him anytime soon, which is a relief at least but is he hedging his bets and keen to keep me onside, should the rest of them make their moves and claim their own inheritance? Like his brothers, is he just playing a game and doesn't really think of me the same way I think of him?

One thing's for sure, I'm walking into Dream Valley with

my eyes wide open, because if I sense one thing out of place, I'm leaving and running home after swearing off men for life.

~

THE REST of the evening is magical. There is something intoxicating about dancing under a glass-domed ceiling with the stars twinkling overhead, in the arms of a man you have only dreamed of finding. Jake doesn't put a foot wrong in either the dance or his easy conversation, and if he is playing a game, I'm enjoying every minute of it.

I often see Sammy in Marcus' arms as they dance under the stars and to outsiders, they seem happy and in love. Part of me thinks that if anyone can make him fall in love with them, Sammy can and she has two years to make it happen. I wonder if he's half way there already because from the look on his face, he likes her more than he's letting on. Then I see the ring catch the light and feel a little envious that she has found purpose and a magical time ahead.

As Jake holds me tenderly in his arms, he whispers, "I'm glad I came because I found you. This ship really has lived up to her name, don't you think?"

As I stare into his gorgeous eyes, I smile. "Only time will tell but I'm looking forward to the future more than I was when I arrived."

As our lips connect, it feels so right. Finally, I've met the man who fits, at least I think he does.

EPILOGUE
ONE MONTH LATER

The car reaches the top of the hill and we both sigh in delight.

"Wow, Jake wasn't kidding, this place is amazing."

Stretching before us like the finest watercolour landscape is a land that received every one of Nature's blessings. Green undulating hills stretch for miles against a backdrop of a sparkling sea. Little tiny buildings nestle inside valleys and the sun is bright as it warms our spirits and provides warmth for the livestock who graze in the lush fields. Wild flowers line the grassy banks and as new homes go, this one is the finest.

"I can't believe we're finally here. It's amazing."

Sammy Jo sounds happy, dreamy even, and I know she is keen to begin this new adventure. "Is it far?"

I squint at the Sat Nav. "Four miles, not long now."

We pass a sign welcoming us to Dream Valley and I think back on how much my life changed since the cruise.

That final week was the most amazing week of my life. I spent most of it with Jake, who couldn't have been better company if he tried. He was fun, attentive and the perfect companion and a delicious shiver passes through me when I think we'll be reunited in less than thirty minutes.

Today we are heading to Valley House. The home of the Hudson brothers and their mother, Camilla. We are about to meet Sammy Jo's future mother-in-law and perhaps mine in the future if things work out with Jake.

Sammy sighs, "Do you think it will be ok?"

"I'm sure of it. How do you feel about meeting Marcus again? Do you feel nervous at all?"

"I'm looking forward to it." She shrugs. "If anything, I'm worried about what his mother will think. Do you think she knows about our, um, arrangement?"

"Jake says no and we're not to say anything. One thing I've learned is the guys dote on their mother and want her to be happy."

"Yes, Marcus told me that in her company we must appear like any newly engaged couple planning a wedding."

"And you're still ok with that?"

Sammy nods. "I am. You see, Marcus is perfect for me, he just needs to work that out for himself."

"You do know you can back out; you don't have to go through with it."

"Coming from the bride who jilted her groom at the altar."

"With very good reason."

She laughs. "Did you manage to catch up with him when you returned, I never asked?"

Since we returned, I've hardly seen Sammy Jo. We've both been busy sorting our lives out and tying up any loose ends ready for our move to Dream Valley.

"Yes, I called him and we met at the Red Robin for lunch one day."

"Did he bring *her*?"

"No, thankfully. Apparently, she thought it was best we met alone, to settle the past and move on."

"She was probably just worried you would slap her. I know I would."

I laugh out loud. "What, slap the woman who did me a huge favour. I'd probably hug her instead and swap friendship bracelets or something."

Sammy laughs. "So how was it, did it feel strange seeing him again?"

"It did. The thing that struck me the most was how much of a stranger he was. It had only been a little over two weeks and yet when I saw him again, it was as if we were old acquaintances and nothing more."

"That's good then."

"Yes, maybe it's because it felt as if I had been away for months because so much happened. When we returned, home seemed different somehow and made my decision easier."

"Did you tell him?"

"Yes. I said I was making a fresh start and moving on. He was surprised but seemed happy for me, probably because he won't have to face me in the street and see me around town."

"So how did you leave things?"

"I handed the ring back, at his request." I pull a face as she says in a shocked voice, "Wow, he really asked for that back. I would have told him I tossed it into the sea in a fit of rage."

I nod. "The thought did cross my mind, but then again I don't really want any reminder of him, anyway. No doubt he'll sell it to buy his new wife a car or something."

"Was it that expensive, I never knew?"

"I think so. He told me it cost three months' salary, and he was on a good wage."

"Then I would definitely have kept it as payment for the emotional trauma he put me through."

Her own rings sparkles as she grips the wheel and I sigh. I don't like to think of Sammy entering into a marriage contract for monetary gain, which is exactly what will happen if Marcus calls time on their arrangement. I really hope not, for her sake and hope that a miracle will happen and Marcus will fall desperately in love with my friend and realise he can't live without her. Then again, it *would* be a miracle because the tales Jake tells me about his brother don't make for happy listening.

Sammy says with interest. "So, did you tell him about Jake? I would have loved to see the look on his face when you told him you had met someone already."

"I didn't. The less he knows about me, the better. I never want to see him again and he doesn't have the right to know my plans."

"Good for you."

"Do you know, he even wanted me to write a note to all the guests to apologise and give him half the money for everything he paid out for, which wasn't much because my parents paid for most of it."

"You were right to jilt him, Florrie; the man's a monster."

I have to agree with her because there wasn't a shred of remorse or even a sorry for marrying somebody else behind my back and not even telling me.

"So, how did it end?"

"I gave him the ring back and told him I was glad I was leaving and would never have to see him again. He just shook his head sadly and said that it was for the best, and he was happier now than he'd ever been. Honestly, the man is a monster. He was so patronising, telling me I may be angry now, but one day I would meet someone and know it was for the best. He even told me not to cling onto the memory of him because it would hold me back from finding anyone else."

Sammy rolls her eyes. "It's his new wife I feel sorry for, she's stuck with the creep. What did your parents say when you told them about Jake?"

There's an awkward silence, and she says incredulously, "You did tell them about him, didn't you?"

"No." I exhale sharply. "How could I tell them I'd already met someone so quickly? All I said was I'd accepted a job and was moving in with you. I told them I needed a fresh start, and they were happy for me. I'll fill in the details when I've had time to settle down and see where this is going with Jake. Do you think I did the right thing?"

I feel anxious because I hated lying to my parents, but it felt wrong at the same time. I'm not sure if they would have understood and Sammy says firmly, "They will only want you to be happy. I'm sure that when they see you together, it will put their minds at rest. You know, we are luckier than most because we have an exciting future ahead of us. I just hope it all works out and Dream Valley really is the promised land."

As we pass through some large gates, the sign tells us we have reached Valley House and I stare at the future with my eyes wide open. Maybe not everyone gets a second chance at finding happily ever after, but I kind of think I have found mine. Sammy Jo, I'm not so sure, but miracles do happen and we will need all the fairy godmothers in existence to work their magic in her case. At least she'll have a friend to pick up the pieces or congratulate her. If you can't find love, a friend is a very close second and my relationship with her will never change.

As we drive towards our future, I'm full of hope for what lies ahead of us and Dream Valley and the Hudson brothers could be the pot of gold at the end of two extremely long overdue rainbows.

Thank you for reading.

Cruising in Love introduces my exciting new Dream Valley series. Find out what happens to the Hudson brothers, not to mention Sammy Jo and Florence.

Sammy Jo's story is up next and we discover just how she deals with being Marcus's fake fiancée. Will it be happily ever after for them, or is that with someone else entirely?

Coming Home to Dream Valley

IF YOU LIKED THIS STORY, you may like Fooling in Love.

WHEN RACHEL DISCOVERED her fiancé was cheating, she did more than just walk away.

Heading to the small, sleepy seaside town of Perivale, Bluebell cottage was the perfect place to stop and think.

Surrounded by nature and simple pleasures, Rachel discovered a life that was very different from her high-powered one in London.

Her new life wasn't without its complications and she was soon distracted by her brooding neighbour, Logan, and the cheeky local handyman, Jack. One she hates with a passion and one she has a passion for.

But life at Bluebell cottage was not all sea, sand, and sunshine because soon the storm clouds roll in and her new life is threatened.

Can Rachel save Bluebell cottage and her new life before the paint has even dried on her 'New Home' sign and is there really such a thing as happily ever after, anyway?

A sweet & light-hearted romance for fans of romantic comedy and starting over.

A story of friendship, relationships, and finding a place where you belong.

Fooling in Love

BEFORE YOU GO

Thank you for reading Cruising in Love.
If you liked it, I would love if you could leave me a review, as I must do all my own advertising.
This is the best way to encourage new readers and I appreciate every review I can get. Please also recommend it to your friends as word of mouth is the best form of advertising. It won't take longer than two minutes of your time, as you only need write one sentence if you want to.

Have you checked out my website? Subscribe to keep updated with any offers or new releases.

sjcrabb.com

When you visit my website, you may be surprised because I don't just write Romantic comedy.

I also write under the pen names M J Hardy & Harper Adams. I send out a monthly newsletter with details of all my releases and any special offers but aside from that, you don't hear from me very often.

If you like social media please follow me on mine where I am a lot more active and will always answer you if you reach out to me.

Why not take a look and see for yourself and read Lily's Lockdown, a little scene I wrote to remember the madness when the world stopped and took a deep breath?

Lily's Lockdown

More books by S J Crabb

<u>The Diary of Madison Brown</u>
My Perfect Life at Cornish Cottage
My Christmas Boyfriend
Jetsetters
More from Life
A Special Kind of Advent
Fooling in love
Will You
Holly Island
Aunt Daisy's Letter
The Wedding at the Castle of Dreams
My Christmas Romance
Escape to Happy Ever After
Cruising in Love
Coming Home to Dream Valley
New Beginnings in Dream Valley

sjcrabb.com

STAY IN TOUCH

You can also follow me on the Social media below. Just click on them and follow me.

Facebook

Instagram

Twitter

Website

Bookbub

Amazon

Printed in Great Britain
by Amazon